The Seton Secret

Frank R. Faunce

Frank R. Faunce

Joe C. Rudé

2.

For more information about *The Seton Secret*, its characters, the book's authors, and other works, visit the author website at

www.frankfaunce.com

Cover design by Mike McDowell

Interior design by Kerry Faunce

ISBN-13: 978-1986446846
ISBN-10: 1986446840

FOREWORD

This book is the sequel to our first book, *The Mystery At The Thirteen Sycamores*. It is the second of a series of books about the history of the Hospitaller Order of Saint John of Jerusalem, but in a novel form. Actually, this project began as a book documenting the history of the Order and its modern branches from its inception about the year 1050 AD as a hospice in Jerusalem. It officially became a military Order after the first Crusade under the auspices of the Crusader Kingdom of Jerusalem. The pope subsequently recognized it and later the other two Crusading Orders—the Knights Templar and later the Teutonic Knights. These Orders participated in many epic battles of the later Crusades defending the Kingdom of Jerusalem and the Holy Land. Eventually, they all met defeat at the hands of the Muslims in 1291 AD.

Shortly thereafter, the Knights Templar were outlawed under the Inquisition in 1307 AD and either joined the other Orders or simply changed their name under the protection of the German, Spanish or Portuguese kingdoms. The Hospitallers followed their own destiny to the island of Rhodes and then Malta, playing a large role in defeating the attempts of Islamic domination of Western Europe. Malta was its last home base until the invasion of Napoleon's fleet and army in 1798 on its way to Egypt. The Hospitaller Knights of Malta then disbursed to their respective countries (langues), never again to be a unified force.

The Scottish branch of the Hospitaller Knights with its embedded Templars hiding under the mantle of the Hospitallers were protected by the Scottish Crown until the Reformation drove them both under the cover of the Scottish Rite Freemasons. As the old Irish saying quoted in our first book goes, "I realized fear one morning at the blare of the fox hunter's sound, when they're all chasing after the poor bloody fox, it's better to be dressed as a hound!"

The secret society aspect of the Templars and the

Hospitallers in Scotland has been the most difficult to research. They were well hidden—the Templars first from the Inquisition and then the Templars and the Hospitallers by the Reformation. At those times, to be discovered was potentially a death sentence! Many Huguenots in France and Catholics and some Separatists in the British Isles died because of their religious beliefs. However, this period is in many ways also the most interesting since it is truly a detective story. Attempting to piece together events relating to secret societies is a formidable task. Subsequently, the Scottish branch of the Order of Saint John with its hidden Templar brothers joined reluctantly to the Orange movement in 1797 and spread to Canada with its members in the Irish and Scottish regiments which formed permanent encampments in 1841. And then the Order spread to the United States in 1874 with many American military members such as admirals Perry and Byrd who planted the Order's flag along with the United States flag at the North and South poles, respectively. This Order gained recognition from the United States Congress and has many members in the military and in the healing arts.

Tracing the history of the Order has involved multiple trips to Europe—Scotland, England, Germany, France and the Middle East—researching their national libraries and exploring multiple historic sites and hidden locations in the countryside.

After ten years of research, we finally sat down to write the convoluted history of the Order of Saint John, and then we realized that a simple history would reach only a few while an adventure novel containing historical facts intertwined with a mystery would appeal to a broader base of readers.

Our first book, *Mystery at the Thirteen Sycamores*, introduced a cast of characters and events related to actual places, people and historical occurrences mixed with adventures that could occur and have occurred in the past. As it has been said, "The past is merely a prelude to the future." Already, events that we supposed could occur in the first book have occurred! All things are possible. Now, our cast of characters have moved on to further adventures in our second book, *The Seton Secret,* and will continue further in our third book currently being written, *Washington's Doubloon*.

We sincerely hope you enjoy this our second book and look forward to the future adventures of our characters. The story lines are, of course, fictional, but are based on factual history and real people and places where we have been. We hope our stories will induce you to do your own research into the history behind our books. Beware of falsehoods woven into the internet histories to push any particular political agenda. Painstaking careful research will separate the wheat from the chaff, but most importantly, have fun and enjoy the story and adventures of the characters and places.

Joe C. Rude'
Atlanta, Georgia, U.S.A.

PREFACE

This book, which is a sequel to *"Mystery at the Thirteen Sycamores,"* is crafted on carefully documented research. There really are Christian Chivalric Orders in existence today that continue the legacy of the original medieval crusading Orders. The first of the three original Orders was the Hospitaller Order of Saint John of Jerusalem that was formed right after the fall of Jerusalem to the Crusaders in July 1099 and still exists in many countries. Later, in 1120, the Poor Knights of the Temple of Solomon in Jerusalem, (the Knights Templar) was founded and survived after their suppression in 1307, hidden within the Order of Saint John in Scotland, Ireland, and Germany. In Spain and Portugal they became the Order of Christ protected by the monarchies of those countries. The third Order that was created in Acre in the Levantine in 1190 was the Order of the Brothers of the German House of Saint Mary in Jerusalem. It was commonly known as the Teutonic Order and still exists in Austria, Belgium, Czech Republic, Germany, Italy, Slovakia, and Slovenia.

The Knights Templar were suppressed in 1307 because of the jealousy and avarice of the French King Philip IV. King Philip IV terrified the weak French Pope Clement V, who was his vassal and forced to live in Avignon, France, rather than the Vatican in Rome. He was virtually surrounded by the king's army.

The king was called "the fair" because of his good looks, not his judgement. He had willing accomplices in other monarchs who also coveted the Templars' treasure. Unfortunately for them, when the Templars' various headquarters in Europe were raided, no treasure was found. The only countries where their headquarters were not challenged were Switzerland, Germany, and Scotland! Even their main headquarters in Paris, the Temple, later demolished by Napoleon, was empty of treasure. The eighteen ships of the Templar fleet that had been anchored in the harbor of La

Rochelle, France, with the treasure had simply vanished!

The Grand Master of the Templars, Jacques de Molay, had previously landed in Marseilles with much fanfare and display of wealth brought from their main base in Crete just a few months before their arrest. After landing in Marseille, their fleet sailed with their treasure through the Straits of Gibraltar and anchored in the port of La Rochelle on the west coast of France, only to disappear on the morning of the mass arrests of the Templars within France on Friday, October the thirteenth, 1307. It simply vanished with rumors that twelve of the ships were going to the excommunicated nation of Scotland and the other six ships going to someplace called New Jerusalem.

Taking great risk, Pope Clement V called for Catholic Inquisitions to investigate the charges laid by Philip, the Fair, against the Templars. The German kingdoms dismissed the charges, they were ignored by Switzerland and Scotland, considered by England, and generally ridiculed by Italy, Portugal, and Spain. The captive pope in Avignon ordered the properties of the Templars to be turned over to the Templars' rival Order, the Hospitaller Order of Saint John, also headquartered in Crete and where they were planning the invasion of Rhodes (which they later conquered). The remaining Templars not arrested were ordered to join the Knights Hospitaller or the other monastic military orders. The pope in August 17-20, 1308, in the Chinon Parchments, declared Templar Grand Master Jacques de Molay and his officers innocent of heresy and absolved them of the lesser charges that had been levied by Philip IV in 1307.

On March 22, 1312, Clement V, under pressure from Philip IV and his smear campaign, issued the bull "Vox in Excelso," which dissolved the Order of the Knights Templar. The pope never issued an order of condemnation against the Order. The suppression was not justified by canon law, but by the necessity of the church and the pope's survival. By 1314, the king of France aggressively intimidated the now dying pope for a decision on the fate of the Templar grand master and his leaders. The pope, unable to deal with the matter, turned it over to a commission of bishops who decided on life imprisonment under church custody. After hearing the sentence of life imprisonment, Grand Master de Molay and his Preceptor of Normandy, Geoffrey de Charny, refused to accept the sentence, proclaiming the Order's absolute innocence.

King Philip IV was incensed and he mounted a massive campaign of misinformation and obscene rumors of immorality against the Knights Templar that were spread like wildfire across Europe by agents of the king. These false stories created scorn and demonstrations by the public. The church tried to counter the false stories by the incontrovertible proof of the Templars' innocence. However, the damage was done and the king of France, on March 18, 1314, illegally seized Grand Master de Molay and Preceptor de Charny from the custody of the bishop's commission and took them to the Isle de France in the Seine River, overlooked by the Notre Dame Cathedral, and burned them at the stake. The somber audience witnessed the two Templars burn at the stake without any cries, demonstrations, or pleas from the two victims.

Jacques de Molay, when led to the stake, asked that their wrists be untied so they could pray to their patron, the Virgin Mary in whose name the overlooking cathedral was consecrated. After praying, de Molay in a loud voice proclaimed to the crowd the innocence of the Knights Templar and their fidelity to the Christian faith. The crowd of onlookers were moved to riot, but was dispersed by the king's men. According to the poet Geoffrey of Paris, de Molay, before the fires were lit, called upon the king and the pope to meet with them and their fellow Templars, who had been tortured and murdered by the king, to come before Christ and God and be judged for their actions before the year was out.

Clement V died on April 20, 1314, and Philip IV died on November 29, 1314, a few months after the execution of the two Templar leaders. Thus, the story of the Templars, the legend of the Holy Grail of Christ at the Last Supper,

Baphomet, the strange skull supposedly worshipped by the Templars, and the Templars' mysterious treasure and ships which vanished from the port of La Rochelle persist to this day.

Frank R. Faunce

ACKNOWLEDGMENTS

Writing any modern mystery novel that shares real history and facts is sometimes more exciting than fiction. This novel is based on historical information that is relevant in today's world. For this reason we would like to acknowledge a few people who inspired us to write our story.

Col. Oscar Stroh, a retired professor from the United States Army War College on the campus of Carlisle Barracks at Carlisle, PA, and the senior aerial intelligence officer for Gen. Douglas MacArthur during the Korean War, and who was also a Knight Hospitaller, encouraged us to write a series of novels based on the history of the Hospitaller Order of Saint John and their colleagues, the Knights Templar, who were linked in brotherhood since the crusades. That mysterious Order was falsely arrested, suppressed, and tortured on Friday the thirteenth of October 1307 in France. Elsewhere they melted into their brother Order, the Knights Hospitaller, as the Frère Maçon, later known as the Freemasons.

The Chinon Parchment, discovered in September 2001 by Barbara Frale, a paleographer at the Vatican Secret Archives, showed that Pope Clement V had absolved the Knights Templar of all charges against them by the Inquisition. Alas, too late to prevent their ordeal, imprisonment, and suppression, much like falsely accused and imprisoned people today!

We would like to also acknowledge Dr. Fran S. Watkins, who inspired us early on to write these books and to press on whenever we became discouraged. She also was an encouraging line, story, and continuity editor throughout the writing of our books.

We would also like to acknowledge the courtesy and assistance of John A. Valenza, DDS, dean, and William N. Finnegan III, distinguished teaching professor in the dental sciences, and Elizabeth K. Wilson, MS, senior director of development at the University of Texas School of Dentistry at the University of Texas Health Science Center in Houston, as well as Taressa C. Visor, director of PACE-Alumni Affairs, continuing education and events for The Denton A. Cooley, MD, and Ralph C. Cooley, DDS, University Life Center, which is also at the University of Texas Health Science Center in Houston. They and Dr. Allen Gaw, who is a clinical assistant professor at the University of Texas, have been most helpful in providing information essential to the writing of this book.

We would be remiss if we didn't include Col. David Hanson, KH, a retired US Army intelligence officer, in our acknowledgments. He taught us what place real history means today, and was throughout our writings a rigorous and faithful editor. His intelligence and wit kept us on our toes! He was a gentle teacher, strict about accuracy, who was always most supportive during the hardest of times in our writings in this book and our previous book, *The Mystery at the Thirteen Sycamores.*

We would also like to acknowledge the creative abilities and suggestions of Mike McDowell for the cover artwork of our first book, *The Mystery at the Thirteen Sycamores,* and this sequel, *The Seton Secret.*

Kerry Faunce is our patient and wise senior editor who has labored tirelessly to keep us on track and provide the final polish on this book, *The Seton Secret,* and make it ready for publication. We are most grateful for his wisdom and guidance to help us finish this book and provide many suggestions for our next book, *Washington's Doubloon,* which is almost finished. We hope you will enjoy this sequel to our first book, *The Mystery at the Thirteen Sycamores,* in our continuing series and will look forward to our next book, *Washington's Doubloon.*

Respectfully, the authors
Frank R. Faunce
Joe C. Rudé

CONTENTS

The Seton Secret

1 SAINT MARY CHAPEL

When Lt. Colonel Dietrich von Schönfeld, his wife Natalie, and their four-year-old daughter Kira Ann arrived at Saint Mary Chapel, a clear deep blue sky with brilliant sunshine was already pouring down onto Mount Lothian. The thirteen sycamores and the roped off area of Saint Mary Chapel loomed in front of them. Yellow signs around the roped off area declared that the Scottish Heritage Foundation was undertaking a historical excavation of the area and trespassing was not allowed. A shudder went through Dietrich as he looked at the chapel where he had almost met his death five years before while on his honeymoon.

Dietrich was tall, handsome, and had blond hair, bright blue eyes and a wide smile that melted Natalie's heart. He was a fighter pilot in the German Luftwaffe with combat experience in Afghanistan as a squadron leader.

Natalie was also tall, about five feet eight, with captivating hazel eyes and dark brown shoulder length hair that curled around her shoulders. She was a nurse from Prague in the Czech Republic who had met her future husband while interviewing for a job at the Phillips University, Gnießen/ Marburg Hospital in Marburg, Germany, where her husband

1

was born and grew up. She had studied dancing as a youngster and was an expert sailor, skier and gymnast. She was also skilled in water skiing and had won championships in all her pursuits. She was elegant in her appearance and exuberant in her love for her husband and her daughter.

The fresh air of spring was a welcome relief from the harsh winter that was relinquishing its hold on Scotland. The excavation team of graduate students from the University of Edinburgh Archaeology Department had been milling about the chapel site watching Professors Randall Fox and John Browne while waiting for Dietrich, Natalie, and Kira Ann to show up so they could begin the dig.

Randall and his friend, Dr. Browne, a member of the Black Knights of Malta and the Venerable Order of Saint John and an antiquities professor from the University of Edinburgh, had been silently looking at the remains of the chapel's foundation and colorful blue tiled floor.

Dr. Browne broke the silence and remarked to his colleague from the Antiquities Department of the University of Texas, "The design is a nice color of blue."

"Yes, it is," sighed Randall, "It reminds me of the bluebonnets blooming in Texas."

Dr. Browne chuckled under his breath. He was reminded that the Blue Bonnets were the Scots who wore the wide brimmed round berets of blue wool with a white flash indicating they were Jacobites during the time of Bonnie Prince Charlie and the Stewart Rebellion. It was an earlier time when Oliver Cromwell had destroyed the ancient Saint Mary Chapel and many other Catholic edifices in Ireland and Scotland during the Protestant-Catholic wars.

Randall explained to Dr. Browne that Dietrich and Natalie had contacted the Scottish Heritage Foundation and showed them indisputable evidence of a hidden room under a section of the chapel's floor where he believed Templar treasure had been hidden from the time of the Templar Inquisition. This evidence was found in the Seton family archives.

Dietrich's ancestor, a Templar knight named Schönfeld,

had been married to Suzanna De Marét on Thursday, October 12, 1307, and that night he and his wife had been attacked in their wedding bedroom by men of a rival knight in the employ of King Philip Le Bel IV of France. Schönfeld had been severely wounded in the surprise attack and knocked unconscious. His wife was kidnapped and he was left for dead. It was later learned that his wife had been murdered resisting the advances of his rival.

His men-at-arms had resuscitated him, bandaged his wounds and carried him back to their ship after they had learned from questioning one of the king's men they found left behind after being knocked unconscious by Schönfeld during the surprise attack on him. The captured king's man told them he was part of a vanguard of a force the king had ordered to seize the eighteen ships of the Templar treasure fleet anchored at La Rochelle, France. The attack on the Templar Knights and seizure of their treasure was planned for the early morning hours of Friday the 13th of October 1307.

Schönfeld and his fellow knights were part of a group of knights and Templar army that slipped away that night from La Rochelle with the eighteen ships of the Templar fleet loaded with the Order's treasure taken from their vaults on Cyprus. They sailed early that morning before it could be seized by the agents of King Philip. It was known that at least twelve ships and their knights and men-at-arms had made their way to Scotland.

The Seton family archives also noted that the knight Schönfeld had a few years later after arriving in Scotland, married Judith Seaton after learning of his wife's death and how she was murdered. He was gripped with a grief that later turned into a terrible thirst for revenge. Judith was the only one who could control his rage. A personal diary of David Seton was also found in the family archives and it told of a great treasure under Saint Mary Chapel. The mystery was how did it get there and what was it?

David Seton, a Templar within the Order of Saint John in the sixteenth century, was known to have led a group of fellow

Catholic Knights Templar who were descendants of those Knights Templar from the treasure fleet. This secret organization of Knights Templar hidden within the Hospitaller Order of Saint John had been protected by King Robert the Bruce of Scotland during the Inquisition and by the Hospitallers during the later Catholic-Protestant wars. They were a separate secret organization of Knights Templar, integrated as part of the Hospitaller Order of Saint John in Scotland and Ireland known as the Frere Maçon or *"Brother Masons."* Seton's diary hinted there were historical documents and part of the Templar treasure hidden in a secret room beneath Saint Mary Chapel.

The two professors had just finished their conversation when Natalie and Dietrich with Kira Ann in tow pulled their white SLC 300 Mercedes Benz roadster into the driveway of Sam Elliott's farmhouse across the road from the meadow and chapel. Annie and Sam with their children, Brian and Susan, saw them drive up and came out of their house with Sean, their black and white border collie, to greet them.

Fifteen-year-old, freckle-faced Brian and his younger sister, blonde-haired Susan, ran to the car to greet them with Annie and Sam close behind. Kira, who was sitting patiently in her mother's lap, immediately leaned out the window of the roadster and reached her arms toward them. Her hazel-brown eyes sparkled warmly as twelve-year-old Susan embraced her.

Brian, who was two years older than his sister and took after his father, brushed his wavy blond hair from his blue eyes and stood behind her waiting patiently for his sister and Kira to finish hugging each other before offering a hesitant "Hello."

Natalie smiled at the children as she opened the roadster's door. Kira jumped out of the roadster, brushing her shoulder length dark brown hair back from her face with her hand as Susan picked her up and turned toward her brother who awkwardly shook Kira's outstretched hand.

Susan, with her long blonde hair, blue eyes and slightly freckled face resembled her mother, and Brian, who was tall for his age, was very quiet but smiled widely at his sister and her newfound friend.

Dietrich had already come around the car and was helping his wife out of the roadster when Sam came over to them to help.

Natalie embraced Sam while Annie hugged Dietrich, looked at Natalie and said, "We are so glad to see you both again and meet your darling daughter."

Natalie turned toward Annie and blurted out, "You mean your goddaughter!"

They all smiled and shook hands while the children finished embracing each other in instant friendship as children are inclined to do.

Sam watched all of this and mused to himself, "If only adults behaved the same way!"

Annie motioned to the children and whispered into Brian's ear, "Would you mind walking the girls back to the house and watch over them while all of you play?"

Brian smiled and puffed out his chest at the responsibility that had been thrust upon him and replied willingly, "Yes, ma'am!"

The children disappeared into the farmhouse with Brian shepherding his wards and the two girls holding each other's hands.

Annie brushed her long, softly curled, blonde hair from her right eye and turned her gaze back to her husband and their friends. She grasped Sam's hand, and put her arm around Natalie's waist. With Dietrich leading the way, they walked up the hill toward the chapel.

Randall and Dr. Browne had also spotted them and were starting to walk down the hill toward the reunion when Annie's dog, Sean, broke out into a full run toward the two professors, wagging his tail furiously in greeting. As he reached Randall, he jumped up into his arms as though he expected the professor to catch him. They were both surprised as Randall snatched him in midair just in time for Sean to lick his friend's face, and then they both fell backward into the lush grass of the meadow.

By this time, everyone had caught up with this merry

5

reunion of old friends and they began shaking each other's hands and embracing. Dr. Browne was caught up in all this merriment as Sean raced in circles around them all.

Dr. Browne's team of graduate students had been watching the action and were smiling at each other in amusement at the behavior of their professor and his colleague. They realized that this dig was going to be more enjoyable than they had thought and maybe these professors were going to be fun after all!

Dietrich and the two professors caught up with the graduate students who were going to uncover the secret room under the chapel. Dietrich had brought the drawings of the old chapel and the photographs that Sgt. John Smedley of the Temple Police had taken of the scene of the attempted assassination of Dietrich.

It was on that terrible morning when Dietrich had just finished sweeping the area of the chapel's floor shown to him by the lens catching the sun's rays at the exact moment of the Venus eclipse of the sun. The sun's image on the floor had revealed the location of the entrance to the hidden room under the chapel. That was when he had been struck down by Mohammad al Hussaini's dagger.

Fortunately, the crime scene pictures taken by Smedley that morning captured the image of the floor that Dietrich had cleared. It was in this area they needed to focus their attention.

The students and Dietrich, along with the professors, walked over to the area seen on the photograph. After several minutes of sweeping, the area where the hidden door in the floor of the chapel was supposed to be was cleared. The two professors accompanying Dietrich got down on their knees, trying to find the outline of the opening.

After examining the tiled floor for a few minutes and not finding any sign of a door, Dietrich shook his head and said, "I don't understand it. I'm positive this is the area that I cleared. It's supposed to be here!"

He got up and walked over to Natalie who was standing next to Annie and Sam beside one of the sycamore trees.

Randall was still standing in the area where the opening to the hidden room was supposed to be and was patiently patting Sean's head. He walked over to Dr. Browne and said, "Why do you think that cleared area is exactly in the middle of the chapel?"

Dr. Browne looked surprised at the remark and said that the chapel was small and the angle of the sun's rays coming in the Venus window on the east would shine on the central aisle leading to the alter which would be wider than the side aisles. About that time, he noticed that Sean was sniffing around the cleared area and was walking in a circle where the spot of the opening was supposed to be.

Dietrich was casually watching them when Dr. Browne snapped his fingers. "It's a circular opening with a stairwell that has purposely been covered over with a door covered by the ceramic tiling. Sean has found the door and is sniffing around its circumference. He has detected the stale air coming from the chamber. All we have to do is carefully remove the tiles to uncover the opening."

Dietrich exclaimed for everyone to hear, "Doc, you're a magician!"

Dr. Browne motioned to two of the more muscular male students to remove the tiles where Sean had been sniffing. After the tiles in the circular area were removed, they could all see a carefully circumscribed circular cut door in the stone with a large round recessed brass loop in its center. The brass loop had a half-moon shaped grip with an emblem of a chevron with a small circle just below the point of the chevron. They could just make out two recessed brass hinges and an indentation in the floor on the west side of the opening that was carefully cut and fitted perfectly into the stone. When the area was cleared, they saw that it was anchored on one side by the hinges so that when a pole was inserted through the circular brass ring and the end of the pole was placed in the cut indentation, a lever was created allowing the circular stone door to be easily raised.

The two men hurriedly put a steel rod through the loop and

raised the stone. Suddenly, stale air from the past escaped the opening and they could see a circular stone stairway and railing leading down into a dark room that no one had entered for centuries.

Everyone stopped and took a deep breath and then Dietrich shouted, "Wow, it's really there!"

When reality had finally sunk in, everyone smiled. Randall looked at his colleagues and Dr. Browne and exclaimed, "We have some torches for everyone!"

He started for the stairway when Randall warned, "Careful, let's take it easy. We don't know how stable those stairs are."

One of the graduate students, George, said, "Wait a minute, we're younger and getting paid to take chances, you are not. I'll go first."

George put a rope around his waist and handed the other end to his fellow student, Archie. "Here, attach this to the circular stone door and hold onto this in case the stairway fails. Hand me that torch and I'll go down. Steady now."

With that, he slowly and carefully descended the stairs until he reached the bottom. Everyone could hear an echo of his breathing heavily as he wandered into the ancient underground room filled with cobwebs. He returned to the bottom of the stairs and shouted up to everyone that the room was big and contained a lot of stuff. He continued and said they would need to rig some lighting before anyone else came down.

With that, Dr. Browne said, "I'll come down with you and help you carefully rig the lights so that nothing is disturbed until we can photograph and document everything."

Everyone instantly concurred and Dr. Browne and Archie descended the stairs while Randall and Dietrich retrieved some lights and electrical cable to hook up to the generator that was part of their equipment cached in the tent outside the chapel where all of their stores were kept.

After the lights were turned on, Dietrich and Randall went down the stairway and when they looked around, they were amazed at what they saw.

Dietrich slowly walked up the stairs to his anxiously waiting wife and friends and he reverently bowed his head as he said, "It's wonderful. You must come down and see it!"

Annie and Sam looked at each other, took a deep breath and smiled at Natalie. Natalie smiled back and carefully stepped down the stairs holding onto the railing and brushing the cobwebs aside with her handkerchief that she was waving like a wand. Annie and Sam followed along behind her with Annie waving her scarf to brush away any cobwebs eluding Natalie. The other students followed behind them anxiously.

When they had all descended the stairs, they assembled into a circle with Randall, Dr. Browne, and Dietrich standing in the middle. George, who had entered the chamber first, looked around the lighted room where he saw numerous boxes, old chests with wrought iron fastenings and locks, several ancient suits of armor with white shields emblazoned with red Maltese crosses upon them, stacked lances, pikes, and swords. There were several ancient lanterns and barrels strewn around the cold, stone floor of the chamber.

George coughed, cleared his throat, looked at Dietrich and then said, almost in a whisper, "What are we looking for, sir?" Dietrich looked around the circle, winked at Natalie and then calmly said, "The Holy Grail."

2 THE HIDDEN ROOM

Everyone could see the large variety of Templar artifacts, weaponry, chests, and boxes neatly lined up. In the middle of it all was a large, lead-covered chest exactly as it had been described in the diary of Dietrich's ancestor, the Templar knight known simply as Schönfeld. It also matched the descriptions found in the Seton library and Archives.

Dietrich turned to Randall, Dr. Browne, the students, and then to Natalie, Annie, Sam, and a panting Sean, and barely breathed the words again, "The Holy Grail." He paused, pointed to the large lead covered chest and breathed, "It must be in there."

They all gathered around the chest and watched as Dietrich pulled on the large double-keyed lock holding the chest's lid in place. To their surprise, the lock opened and fell to the floor with a ringing thud.

"It's unlocked!" gasped Natalie as she covered her mouth with her hand. "How can that be?"

Randall who had been silently watching, exclaimed, "It looks like somebody was in a hurry and just forgot to lock it back up!"

"Either that or they didn't want to lock it. Let's see what's inside," volunteered Dr. Browne

Dietrich hesitantly grabbed the handle on the top of the chest and carefully lifted the lid as the ancient hinges creaked. When the lid was laid back, they all peered inside and with one voice exclaimed, "It's empty!"

"Not quite," Randall, said slowly as he pointed his flashlight into the chest. "There's a large leather-covered book back in the corner. I wonder why it was left."

He took his camera and carefully photographed the chest and its contents.

Dietrich then reached into the chest to grab the book and Dr. Browne grabbed his arm and firmly said, "Wait, put these white gloves on. We don't want to damage this ancient manuscript!" He paused and then he continued, "And besides it's covered with dust and we don't want to get your hands dirty."

And then he laughed. His comrades immediately laughed and the tension was broken.

Dietrich immediately put the gloves on and reached into the chest and retrieved the tome. Natalie lowered the lid of the chest and Dietrich placed the book on top where everyone could see. As he opened the book, it became apparent that it was very old and written in ancient German. There was a letter folded and with a wax seal lying on top of the first page of the book.

By now, Dr. Browne had handed white gloves to everyone and was intently peering at the seal with a magnifying glass. He stammered, "It—it's the Seton family coat of arms! What is it doing with a much older book written in fourteenth century German?"

He took his camera from the pocket of his jacket and snapped a couple photographs of the letter *in situ*. Then he carefully picked it up and silently read the contents of the letter that was written in sixteenth century English, rather than Scottish.

After he finished, he had an ashen look on his face and said,

"I need to decipher this. It is difficult to read." Then he mysteriously put his right forefinger to his lips and smiled at Randall who was watching him intently.

Randall winked back at Dr. Browne and said, "Let's carefully place this book and letter in a plastic bag so we can look at them later in a more studious manner."

Dr. Browne then turned to Natalie and Dietrich and said, "Let's carefully photograph and mark every item in this chamber and package them for transport to our laboratory in Edinburgh University where they can be studied and photographed in an environment that won't damage them. George and his fellow students are specially trained to package and load these artifacts into the lorries outside and then secure the site from vandals or curious onlookers. Randall, Dietrich, you and I will take custody of the book, manuscripts and letter and transport them to our special laboratory at the university."

And then he winked at Randall.

Dietrich and Randall nodded in agreement as they began their task of securing the artifacts.

Natalie whispered to Dietrich, "He's found something."

Dietrich nodded his head in agreement and they went about their tasks with Randall, Dr. Browne, and his students cataloguing and photographing everything in place before it was numbered, packaged, moved to the lorries, and secured for transport.

After the work was complete and the site secured, Randall, Dr. Browne, Annie, Sam, Natalie, and Dietrich watched as George and his fellow students drove away toward Edinburgh and the University. Dr. Browne had kept the book and letter in his possession.

3 AT THE FARM HOUSE:
THE SECRET

The intrepid band looked at each other, sighed in relief, turned, and then walked down the hill with Sean, their border collie and friend, toward the farmhouse and the children. Reaching the farmhouse with their book, manuscripts, and the letter, the children greeted them with big hugs all around. Kira had long brown hair and hazel eyes that twinkled as she spoke, mimicking her mother's eyes. She was wearing a bonnie blue cotton dress with a white sash and bow in the back covering some white leggings that now had some scuff marks on the knees.

When they entered the living room, she pointed to the table where a puzzle with the map of Scotland was lying. She looked up to her parents with a satisfied expression on her face and happily said, "Mommy, daddy, they showed me how to work a puzzle! Come see what we've done" as she dragged them toward the table.

Brian and Susan were smiling as Brian looked at Natalie and Dietrich and his sister and proudly said, "She did it all by herself—well almost! She even knew what the map of Scotland looked like."

Dietrich looked admiringly at his wife and daughter and exclaimed, "She ought to; she's been reading about Scotland and studying its map for over a week!"

"Daddy, mommy helped me." she triumphantly announced.

Randall winked at Dr. Browne who said, "She's going to be a scientist, you know—she knows how to solve puzzles."

With that, he put on some white cotton gloves and drew the letter that he had silently looked at and said, "Can everyone keep a secret? I know that you are all aware that I don't really have to take this to my laboratory to read it. I just wanted to keep this between us. Annie, Sam, what I am about to say must remain a secret; otherwise, it could be dangerous to everyone who knows. I think it might be a good idea for the children to play in a bedroom for a few minutes while I explain what *we* have discovered."

And he emphasized the "we."

Annie and Natalie looked at their children and explained that they were going to have an adult talk and that they were going to have to play a game or watch television in the bedroom.

Kira clapped hands and exclaimed, "Good, let's watch television, I have to read books at home!"

Natalie smiled, then looked at Annie who nodded her approval and then she said to Kira, "Okay, your godmother has said 'yes,' but remember this is only what you and your brother and sister also agree to watch. Now, all of you hurry along."

Annie escorted them to Sam and her bedroom and closed the door with the admonishment, "Not too loud, now."

Then she returned to the living room where Dr. Browne took the letter out, looked at everyone and said, "The leatherbound book was written by the German knight, Schönfeld and is his autobiography. The letter was written by David Seton in 1572."

Then he began to read the ancient letter and simultaneously

translate it out loud in modern English. The letter said,

"Let it be known to all who have found this chamber beneath the Holy Floor of Saint Mary Chapel, that these stores have been left to defend what remains of the last of the Poor Knights of Christ of the Temple of Solomon who have been protected as Fréres Maçons within the protection of the Knights of the Hospital in Scotland since the time of the Inquisition begun by King Phillip IV of France and his puppet, Pope Clement V on Friday the 13th of October 1307 during his theft of the Templar properties in France. The Knights of the Temple sailed for Scotland with twelve of the eighteen ships of the Order from the fleet anchored at La Rochelle and with the brave knight Schönfeld left for dead in his wedding chamber after his bride, Suzanna De Marét was stolen and later murdered by henchmen of the criminal Phillip IV. The king sought to capture the fleet of eighteen ships holding the treasure of the Knights of the Temple withdrawn from the Temple vault in Cyprus prior to coming to France at the time of the arrests on the 13th of October 1307. The treasure of the twelve of the ships of the Templars has been moved from this place to New Jerusalem by Earl Henry Saint Clair, Prince of Orkney in 1396 whereas the previous six ships with its treasure sailed on to New Jerusalem from La Rochelle at the time of the arrests. Only the Holy Grail, the skull of our Order and the sword of Schönfeld has been left for us to return them to their Holy Place."

Dr. Browne looked at his audience after he finished reading and could see that they were amazed at the contents of the letter. He added, "Below the writing there is a chevron with a small circle under the point."

Then he held the manuscript up so everyone could see the emblem.

Randall cradled his chin in his left hand thoughtfully and then said, "Dietrich, what happened to your ancestor Schönfeld after he survived the attack?"

"According to our family records, he fought with the Scots and went on to fight in the Battle at Bannockburn."

Dr. Browne then queried, "Did he ever remarry?"

"Yes, he married Judith Seton."

Dr. Browne raised an eyebrow and then he said, "Then all of this is a Seton Secret! The Setons must have known where the treasure and the Holy Grail along with the skull and Schönfeld's sword are located. Was there anything in their archives to tell us where the sword, grail and skull are?"

Dietrich looked down and muttered, "No, but it's apparent that David Seton took them with him and they left in haste without locking the chest."

Dr. Browne then replied, "The letter indicates that the Templar treasure was taken to some place called New Jerusalem on some ships in 1386 by Henry Saint Clair. This letter signed by David Seton with his seal was written sometime in the 1570s when he and some of the Templars left Scotland after the Grand Prior James Sandilands of the Knights Hospitallers created a thunderstorm by becoming Protestant and befriending John Knox at the Knox Parliament in 1560.

"This later caused David Seton and his small group of Catholic Knights Templar to separate from the now increasingly Protestant Hospitaller Order and Templar Order in Scotland and leave Scotland in 1572 never to return."

Dietrich picked up the conversation, "David Seton had declared at the 1560 Knox Parliament that Hospitaller lands at Torphichen and surrounding Templar lands including those at Temple had been held in trust by the Order of Saint John, Knights Hospitaller, since the Inquisition and the Templar lands and property should be returned to the Templars in Scotland since those lands and property had been handed over illegally to the Scottish Crown by the now Protestant Grand Prior James Sandilands."

Randall then breathed, "Yeah! Along with a title of Lord Saint John that Queen Mary of Guise gave him on January 24, 1563, and then she gave back the Templar land and property with the Hospitaller property as a personal gift to the very same Sir James Sandilands the next day on January 25, 1563."

He continued, "The Catholic Mary of Guise who was regent Queen of Scotland before her daughter Mary became Queen of Scots a year later."

Dietrich said, "I understand that the Torphichen and Templar lands were given to James Sandilands and he and his descendants were given an Earldom and a title of Lord of Torphichen. From that time forward, the Order of Saint John and the Knights Templar in Scotland have been separate from the state. Queen Mary of Guise, I know, wrote to her daughter, Mary, Queen of France, of the affair and that she would keep the secret of the Hospitallers and the Templars in Scotland. After her husband, the King of France, died and her mother died the next year, she became the Queen of Scotland."

Randall raised his eyes and postulated, "Could this secret carried to the grave by Mary of Guise and her daughter Mary, Queen of Scots, refer to the location of New Jerusalem and the treasure of the Templars and the whereabouts of the sword of Schönfeld, the skull, and the Holy Grail?"

Natalie interjected, "Intriguing, isn't it? Let's talk about it later after we've read the book and the manuscripts. They may shed more light on this secret of the Setons."

With that, Annie and Natalie both declared that it was time for them to fix dinner and retrieve their children watching television.

Everyone laughed, and Sam went to get the kids.

4 THE CONFERENCE

At the University of Edinburg, Dr. Browne looked around the conference room in his office and then at the five people sitting around the large oak conference table situated in the middle of the room. The room was paneled with ancient oak and contained a large stained-glass window depicting John the Baptist baptizing Jesus before Peter's younger brother Andrew and saying, "Behold the lamb of God." This prompted Andrew to become the first disciple of Jesus and later bring his older brother Simon Peter into the fold of apostles. Saint Andrew is the Patron Saint of Scotland, Russia, and Greece. The room was lined with glass-enclosed bookcases filled with Dr. Browne's favorite books.

Large crystal glasses were on the table in front of each guest and the traditional decanter of single-malt Scotch whiskey was in the center of the table next to a flask of spring water,

After he was satisfied that everyone was comfortable, Brown cleared his throat, closed the heavy oak door to the room, and said, "I know you are all anxiously waiting to find out what I have discovered which may shed some light on what happened to the treasure and secret contents of the chamber beneath Saint Mary Chapel."

Over in a corner of the room was Kira, dressed in a bright blue flowery dress and white leggings, curled up in a large brown leather chair next to the window reading a book. She was so engrossed she hardly noticed the adults in the room, let alone what they were saying.

Dr. Browne, adjusted his regimental tie, unbuttoned his Harris Tweed jacket, took his place at the head of his conference table, and quietly poured a glass of his favorite Glenlivet Scotch—neat, of course—and invited everyone else to do the same.

Natalie, dressed in a dark green dress with matching jacket, and Katie Grant, looking lovely in a blue skirt and jacket with a white silk blouse, declined his offer, but Randall, Dietrich and Inspector Steve Grant of the Scottish National Security Forces, Katie's husband, eagerly followed Dr. Browne's lead and poured the Scotch into their glasses. The three of them in their sport coats and Windsor knotted ties turned to Dr. Browne after taking a sip of their Scotch.

Randall looked at his friend, Dr. Browne, and said, "Jack, what do you think happened to the treasure and Schönfeld's sword, the Holy Grail, and the skull?"

"Well," Dr. Browne replied, "after looking at some additional information in the Seton family archives, I think the treasure hidden at Saint Mary Chapel definitely did go to New Jerusalem on the fleet of ships that Earl Henry Saint Clair, Prince of Orkney, gathered at the request of Queen Margrette of Norway. She was concerned about the hegemony of the Hanseatic League over trade and shipping in Northern Europe and the Baltic and was determined to open new trade routes around the west coast of Ireland, avoiding the Hanseatic League, to an area she and Prince Henry called the New Jerusalem.

"What is puzzling is that, according to the Seton Archives, the fleet was at least fourteen ships, including galleys, merchant barks and ships armed with cannons, which sailed from the Orkneys without any fanfare and on the evening tide. The ships carried a group of Cistercian monks from Götland,

Templar knights and men-at-arms, as well as goods, baggage, and the rest of the treasure from Cyprus that had been stored since 1307 in the secret chamber at Saint Mary Chapel. The Seton archives also mention a letter sent to Pope Boniface IX in 1395 by Queen Margrette that mentions her concerns about trade with her kingdom and the Hanseatic League. There is a note in the Seton Archives written by Queen Margrette to Prince Henry Sinclair that speaks about her letter to the pope and his response saying that he wished them well on their mission and gave his blessing to their enterprises establishing new trade routes."

Dietrich was sitting silently next to Dr. Browne, and when Randall sat down, he looked down at the table and then up to the professor and then around the table at everyone.

Randall appeared to be in deep thought, and then he said, "Jack, was there any mention in the archives of the contents in the box we found that was unlocked?"

"Not a word," replied Dr. Browne.

"Then, we must assume the box and its contents were left secure and intact at the time the treasure was removed in 1396," Randall murmured.

"Yes, it would seem so," Dr. Browne replied.

Katie was listening patiently to the conversation when she said, "Then we must agree that the box was opened at a later time and at great haste by David Seton in 1570 or 1572 and the contents were removed and taken away before anyone could stop them. The letter we found written by a David Seton has a tone of animosity. Some dramatic event must have occurred that prompted the rapid removal of the grail, skull, and Schönfeld's sword."

"Wait a minute," interjected Steve. "Let's look at this thing carefully. David Seton was the leader of the Catholic Templar contingent within the Order of Saint John and he argued at the John Knox Parliament in 1560 against the taking of the Templar property and lumping it with the Hospitaller property when it was given to Grand Prior Sandilands. I understand that he left Scotland with a group of Knights Templar and their families in 1570-72, never to be seen again. It was rumored that they went to Germany to join up with the Templar Knights who were hiding inside the German Langue of the Order of Saint John. Isn't that correct, Dietrich?"

"Yes," Dietrich agreed. "That is, until that group later became Lutheran."

Randall interjected, "No, the Catholic German Langue remained intact, and later the Lutheran knights of the Bailiwick of Brandenburg with their money were only accepted as associate members, as well as a Greek Orthodox contingent. The Chapel of Our Lady of Philermos is in the Order of Saint John's Co-Cathedral in Malta. It was dedicated to the Virgin Mary and was the first one to be given a particular devotion. It had housed an icon of the Virgin Mary that they believed to be miraculous to help them in their victories. It was Byzantine and they had brought it from Rhodes. After victory, they would bring the keys to the conquered fortresses to the chapel where they remain today. That icon was taken from the island by Grand Master von Hompesch after Napoleon's conquest in 1798 and was lost until it was rediscovered in a monastery in Montenegro. It is now exhibited in the Fine Arts Museum."

Dietrich amended his statement saying, "I meant that the Grand Master Emmanuel de Rohan-Polduc obtained a papal bull in 1782 to revive the English Langue, which included Scotland, Wales, and Ireland. In 1784 Grand Master Emmanuel de Rohan-Polduc with a chapter general reinstituted the Langue as the Anglo-Bavarian Langue with Polish and Bavarian knights."

He continued, "The Polish Grand Priory was expanded to include Russian orthodox knights and a Russian Grand Priory in Saint Petersburg when a treaty was made between the Order and Russia for financial aid to replace their income cut off from France by Napoleon's forces. The pope was surrounded by Napoleon's forces and agreed to the expansion, especially since the Order already had a Greek Orthodox connection from their time on Rhodes. The Catholic German king in Bavaria readily agreed to the Russian expansion by treaty with Russia since Austria was threatening to take over Bavaria and he needed the protection of Russia and Tsarina Catherine II as well as Russian aid. The broker for the deal was an Alsatian knight of the Hospitaller Order of Saint John, Baron Johann Baptiste Anton von Flachslanden, who was captain general of the Order's powerful Mediterranean fleet. It was this fleet that prowled the sea lanes protecting European merchant shipping from the marauding Muslim pirates who would capture their ships and cargo, taking plunder, and selling their passengers and crew in the Middle Eastern slave markets which still exist."

Natalie supported her husband's statement and added, "Then the answer must be in Germany. Maybe the Vatican Secret Archives also would have some documents that would shed some light on the whereabouts of David Seton when he and his fellow Catholic knights left Scotland for Germany. Surely, he must have sought the advice of the pope on the matter of having the Holy Grail and the skull of the Templars!"

Dr. Browne added, "Remember a few years ago when Templar historian Barbara Frale discovered the long lost Chinon Parchment misfiled in the Vatican Secret Archives, a transcript that revealed that Pope Clement V had absolved the Templars of all charges of heresy."

"Yes, and I might point out that Baron von Flachslanden was also the spymaster for the intricate web of spies that the Order maintained throughout the Islamic world and the Ottoman Empire," Randall chimed in. "He was the inside man with the Bavarian king and interceded on Catherine's behalf and arranged for joint naval exercises with the Order's fleet and a safe harbor for part of her Baltic fleet in the Mediterranean."

Dr. Browne reminded everyone that it was this same man who suggested that John Paul Jones be commissioned as an admiral in the Russian navy to help her build a Black Sea fleet after she captured the Ukraine and the Crimean port of Sebastapol.

He quipped, "Thomas Jefferson even endorsed the idea, and on April 23, 1787, the hero of the American Revolution accepted Catherine's offer."

Katie and Steve had been quietly sitting by and silently watching the enthusiastic exchange of information. Katie turned to her husband, winked at him, and then offered a suggestion as she cut to the chase, "I believe Natalie is correct—there is a German connection, but if the pope was involved in 1570 and in 1572, might there be a record or clue of some kind in the Vatican Archives in Rome as well as in Germany?"

Steve smiled and, with an admiring glance at his beautiful wife with her sparkling blue eyes and golden hair, sighed, "I couldn't agree more. What does everyone think about the idea of someone with Vatican credentials checking out the archives and Natalie and Dietrich check out where David Seton and his wife went in Germany."

Dietrich looked at his wife and then said, "Natalie, do you remember something in my family's records about David Seton and his wife being buried in the Church of the Scotch Convent at Ratisbon, or rather Regensburg as it's now known, near Nuremberg?"

"Yes, I think so," she replied. "I believe the records say something about his wife Marjory dying before he died, and feeling great remorse, he went on a journey somewhere and came back to Germany to be close to her. I believe the records say he died ten years after her."

"Aha!" exclaimed, Dr. Browne. "Then George Seton in his history of the Seton family got it wrong when he said that David died in 1581. It was his wife, Marjory, who died then. That clears matters—Whitworth Porter, who had access to the Hospitaller Archives in Valetta, Malta, in 1858 wrote that David Seton was a real person who had been in Malta and later died in Germany in 1591. That clears up the discrepancy and validates Andrew Ramsey's contention about the Seton family and their relation to the Frére Maçon within the Hospitaller Order of Saint John."

"Then, he is probably buried next to his wife," muttered Randall. "Could he then have gone to Malta, and for what reason?"

Natalie replied, "Sounds plausible. Oh, by the way, our cousins, Carolyn and Christopher, have just finished building their Manor House at Loch Moy, and Carolyn called me the other day and said she and Christopher accompanied by their lawyer, Diamond Dave, and his wife Debbie were coming over to Scotland to celebrate the opening of their new house and spend a couple of months in their adopted homeland Scotland. I'm sure they wouldn't mind a few more house guests. They especially mentioned Katie and Steve for the celebration. Perhaps by that time we'll have some information from the Vatican and we can meet again at their house."

Randall added, "I'm sure they will want to meet Professor Browne. They have already called me to be there for the celebration."

"I'll call her to see when they'll be here," Natalie said.

Kira's head popped up out of her book when she heard her mother mention Carolyn and Christoper's names, and a thin voice asked, "When will they be here? Can we stay a while longer here until they arrive? They are such fun!"

Natalie looked at everyone and said, "Yes and they give you anything you want."

Kira looked down at the floor and then sheepishly up at her parents and everyone who was smiling, and with a pouting lip said, "But, I love them both and they love ice cream!"

After everyone had a good laugh at Kira's reply, Dr. Browne looked at his compatriots and said, "Well, I have all the necessary credentials and a pass card to visit the Vatican and their archives. You know they have very strict rules and only carefully selected people, including academics with the necessary academic degrees and backgrounds, are vetted to examine documents in their archives. Once allowed, a person must go through a stringent security check just like at an airport and are only allowed to carry a pencil with soft lead and a paper pad to write on. A cell phone is occasionally allowed if it is turned off. We are only allowed one person at a time and accompanied by an archivist priest to a vaulted area with light, humidity, and temperature controls where you can study with white gloves whatever documents you have applied to study.

"The application for study is carefully investigated and, if accepted, the time allowed is worked out in advance so as not to waste anyone's time. I believe the questions we might be looking to solve are: Does the Vatican have any records of David Seton having a meeting with either Pope Pius V or Pope Gregory XIII after Pope Pius' death on May 1, 1572? We know by a Papal Bull in 1570, Pope Pius V excommunicated Queen Elizabeth I and declared she was not the rightful Queen of England."

Randall had been listening intently and then suggested that maybe Natalie and Dietrich could find out from the Schönfeld or Seton archives why David Seton might have wanted to go to Malta after his wife died.

"There must be a record somewhere," he said.

He continued, "Maybe, David Seton took the relics to Rome to give to the pope. If so, there certainly would be a record of that, and don't forget that Pope Gregory XIII succeeded Pope Pius V on May 13, 1572, and if David Seton left Scotland in 1572, it would probably have been after Pope Gregory XIII had been elected—when the weather would have been warmer and the political climate better for traveling."

Dr. Browne interjected, "Remember that Gregory XIII was a staunch supporter of King Phillip II to dethrone Queen Elizabeth I of England. I believe that David Seton, who was the master of the Templar properties and the remaining treasure entrusted to him for safekeeping within the Hospitaller Order which lay beneath the Saint Mary Chapel, would want to get it out of Protestant and Sir James Sandiland's hands. He and his contingent of Catholic Templars within the Order of Saint John were becoming less and less confident that their best interests were being served by the Hospitaller Order in Scotland which was becoming alarmingly influenced by the reformer John Knox."

Dr. Browne smiled and then said, "I'll make all of the

arrangements to go to the Vatican and see what I can dig up.
And then he laughed—maybe I'll be as lucky as Barbara Frale
with the Chinon Parchment!"

5 THE VATICAN

The sky was remarkably clear with an abundance of sunshine pouring down on the Eternal City of Rome. Dr. Browne, after a good night's sleep at the Albergo del Senato Hotel, walked briskly toward the Porta Sant'Anna entrance to the Vatican Secret Archives where two Vatican City Swiss Guards in their colorful sixteenth century inspired uniforms were checking the credentials of authenticated scholars.

As Dr. Browne approached them with his entry card in hand, one of the guards recognized him from a previous trip two months prior and smiled, greeting him in perfect English, "Good morning Professor Browne, it is a pleasure to see you again."

Dr. Browne nodded his head and replied, "It's indeed a pleasure to see you again, Rafael. It's a beautiful day for enlightenment. How is your wife and your little daughter Anna?"

The guard was startled that Dr. Browne had remembered their conversation two months before when he had researched Mary, Queen of Scots' plea to Pope Sixtus V for her life on November 23, 1586. In her missive, she asked forgiveness for her sins and argued her case against the falsehoods perpetrated by her English persecutors.

Dr. Browne smiled, then waved at the two guards as they permitted him to continue through the Cortile del Belvedere to the research desk where he presented his entry card. His request for a search for any documents describing a visit to Pope Gregory XIII in 1572 by David Seton had been received and he was delighted that such a document had been found and he was to be escorted by a clerk to a reading room where he would be allowed to examine the document concerning David Seton. The escort identified himself as a Vatican priest, Marco Baronio.

"Good Morning Professor Browne," Fr. Baronio said. "Roberto Barberini, who was your clerk two months ago and was looking forward to serving you, has taken ill this morning and I have the pleasure of assisting you. I have an extra paper pad and a newly sharpened lead pencil for you if you require them."

"Thank you very much," replied Dr. Browne. "I have my own pad and pencil in my briefcase and I believe that will be all I need. I appreciate your thoughtfulness."

The priest and the professor walked carefully down the stairs to the underground labyrinth that led to a well-lit reading room where the document lay on a neat, small desk on the far side of the room.

"I'll be right outside the door if you need anything, professor," said his escort who then withdrew from the room.

The document was written in Latin which was the custom of the time in the sixteenth century as it still is in the Vatican. Dr. Browne eagerly put on his white gloves and then began scanning the fragile document.

"There it is!" he exclaimed as he eagerly pulled out his pencil and pad from his briefcase and started to write some notes. He finished writing his notes on the page, which he then tore from the pad, and carefully placed the pad back into his briefcase. He then started to fold the page with his notes to put into his inside coat pocket when he leaned back in his chair and became aware of the priest's presence behind him.

He had just started to take a deep breath of relief before speaking when the priest's left hand swiftly moved past his left ear and an opened plastic bag with a cotton handkerchief soaked in chloroform was pressed over his nose and mouth. The deep breath he had started inhaled the fumes of the anesthetic deeply into his lungs and he could feel a shadow starting to close over his eyes as he heard the priest say, "Allah Akbar" and then he slipped into a dark pool of unconsciousness with the folded note he was holding falling onto the desk.

The priest kept the plastic bag in place as Dr. Browne slumped in his chair. He then loosened Dr. Browne's tie and shirt and pulled his Harris Tweed jacket and shirt back to expose the professor's right shoulder and clavicle. Then he deftly and cautiously withdrew his lead pencil from a plastic box he had laid on the desktop next to Dr. Browne's folded notes. The pencil had been soaked in a hydrogen cyanide solution of 2500 ppm overnight so that the liquid was thoroughly absorbed into the wood and graphite. With gloved hands, the priest precisely stabbed the pencil behind and in the middle of Dr. Browne's right clavicle down to his right subclavian vein so that the deadly poison would enter the vein and travel directly to his heart.

Fr. Baronio was really a Muslim physician trained in Germany and was a member of the Muslim Brotherhood. He had been carefully inserted into the Vatican clerical staff to obey the will of the Brotherhood. He was a "mole" who had done his duty without question.

He estimated that the professor would be dead within a minute, and since any bleeding would be internal, he twisted the pencil, broke off the graphite tip, removed the remainder of the pencil, and put it back into its plastic case. He then buttoned the professor's shirt, tightened his tie, and pulled his coat together so that he was slumped over the desk and appeared to have had a heart attack.

Picking up the notes that Dr. Browne had scribbled, the

plastic case with its deadly pencil, and the plastic bag with the soaked handkerchief, Fr. Baronio ran back to the credentials desk and stammered, "Call…call a doctor and come quickly, I…I think Dr. Browne has had a heart attack!"

The priests at the credentialing desk looked confused at what Fr. Baronio was saying—and then it sank in.

One of the priests picked up a telephone, punched in an emergency number and a woman's voice answered, "What's happened?"

The priest said, "One of the researchers, a Professor Browne has apparently suffered a heart attack and needs help immediately!"

The nun on the other end of the conversation replied, "I have a doctor on the way."

Baronio stammered, "I'll go alert the Swiss guards. You know where the reading room is that Dr. Browne is in, don't you?"

The other priest behind the credentialing desk said, "Yes, I'll show the doctor when he gets here."

"Good," replied Baronio as he ran toward the Cortile del Belvedere. When he reached the guards, he shouted, "They need you inside quick, it's an emergency!"

Then he ran toward the Porta Sant'Anna and disappeared.

The guard, Rafael, turned to his companion and muttered, "I wonder where he's off to?"

About that time, another Swiss guard came running up to them and said, "One of the Secret Archives priests has been found stabbed with a curved Muslim dagger, but he's still alive and babbling something about a Muslim priest and the Muslim Brotherhood."

6 THE SCOTTISH INSPECTOR

Steve Grant was leaning back in his chair in his office, gazing at the soft white clouds gathering in the late afternoon blue skies and dreaming of having a wonderful dinner with his beautiful blonde-haired and blue-eyed wife when suddenly, she popped her head around the edge of his door and said," What are you thinking about?"

He swung his chair around quickly, smiled broadly, and quipped, "There you go again, reading my mind!"

He still could not figure out how she could read his mind almost before he could.

"I know, you're thinking about those steaks and the Glenlivet tonight, aren't you?"

Steve's eyes brightened and he was about to say that she was mistaken when Katharine Sue Winslow Grant suddenly laughed and slowly said, "You're really thinking of me and after dinner aren't you? I can tell by the glint in your eyes."

His face fell as she came over to him and put her arms around his neck and whispered into his ear, "Why don't we have an early dinner and see what we can do about making a pretty baby like Kira Ann?"

His heart melted, he couldn't help it, he kept falling more

31

in love with his wife every day. He thought, "How lucky can I be to wake up and see her every morning!"

Suddenly his telephone rang. Lifting the phone to his ear, he heard the voice of his boss, James Ferguson, the head of Scottish Security say, "Steve, I hate to break the bad news, but your friend Professor Browne has been discovered in the Vatican Secret Archives apparently poisoned. He's dead and they have asked for our help and particularly yours to fly to Rome and help them solve this matter.

"Oh, and yes, I want you to take your pretty wife with you. Together, the two of you are a regular Sherlock Holmes and Dr. Watson; although, I'm not quite sure who is who," he said, laughing. "Have Katie book your flights for around 10 a.m. tomorrow, and we'll give you a briefing about what the Vatican knows before you leave."

Then he hung up.

"What was that all about?"

Steve replied, "Katie, the boss wants us to fly to Rome tomorrow morning and visit the Vatican Police. Our friend, John Browne, has been murdered."

"What! You're kidding—right?"

"No, I'm sorry, darling. It's true. John is dead. He didn't give me the details. I guess he wants us to get a good night's sleep. We'll get the facts he finds out overnight tomorrow morning in a briefing before we leave for the airport."

Katie sighed and then breathed into his ear, "Let's still have an early dinner and go to bed early—okay?"

Morning rolled around too early and Katie put her arm over her husband's chest and kissed him tenderly on his lips and said, "Do you think it will be a boy or a girl?"

Steve raised an eyebrow and winked at Kate and said, "Kate, it will probably be twins."

Katie pulled the covers down to reveal his slender, but muscular and tanned, six-feet-two-inch body with his tousled curly black hair arched over one eye, and then she moved close to him and put her arms around his neck.

She was slender with the body of a beautiful athlete. Her

long, blonde hair curled around her shoulders and breasts like a halo. She whispered into his ear, "As long as he looks like you…" and before she could finish her sentence, he added, "And she looks like you, darling."

He kissed her passionately on her lips. They embraced and picked up their love-making where they had quit the night before.

Before they knew it, time had evaporated and it was time to get out of bed, shower, get dressed, have breakfast, and leave for Steve's office.

They had dropped their clothes on a chair the night before and crawled into bed without bothering to put on pajamas or a nightgown. Steve headed for the shower with Katie following him. They figured that would be faster than showering singly, but somehow it never was.

After breakfast, they brushed their teeth and combed their hair before picking up the travel bags Katie had packed the night before. They climbed into their five-year-old silver Jaguar XF, 240 hp, 2.0 liter, i4 turbocharged four-door sedan that Steve's aunt had bought for him, hoping he would get up the nerve to propose to Katie.

They parked in the parking lot of the Scottish security headquarters and went upstairs to the briefing room to get the information from the Vatican police. During the night, reports had been flowing into their computers from Interpol and the Vatican police about the murder of Dr. Browne and the Muslim agent disguised as a priest who committed the murder and the attempted murder of the priest, Roberto Barberini.

As they entered the briefing room, they could see that something was different. Steve's boss, James Ferguson, wasn't in the room, but the deputy director general at MI5 from Thames House in London, Sir Richard Bothwell, was sitting in a chair smoking a pipe and looking out of a window at the early morning mist covering the horizon. He turned as they entered and he rose from his chair to greet Steve and Katie.

"I'm afraid that our old nemesis, the Muslim Brotherhood is at it again. They managed to get one of their agents into the

Vatican and kill one your friends and a Scottish citizen, Dr. Browne," he said.

"I never had the pleasure of meeting him, but I understand both of you knew him well. We just can't allow this sort of thing happen unpunished, can we?"

Steve looked into Bothwell's steely grey eyes and could see the seriousness in them.

"You know that the queen was a close friend of his and she isn't taking this matter lightly and neither are we! What was he doing in the Vatican?" Bothwell asked.

"Sir Richard, he was trying to find some documents concerning the departure of David Seton from Scotland in 1572," Steve replied. "He said that David Seton was supposed to have an audience with the pope that spring and then he disappeared…I'm afraid with some treasure that was hidden beneath the floor of an ancient chapel—Saint Mary Chapel on Mount Lothian."

"Rather a cold trail for recovery of some of our national treasure, don't you think?" Bothwell asked.

"No, I believe he was onto something and found it. Otherwise, why was he murdered?" Steve replied. "And why is the Muslim Brotherhood involved?"

"I don't know," Bothwell said, "but you and your wife Katharine are now working directly for the queen and she expects this whole affair to be taken care of as quickly as possible. After your successful conclusion of this case, she wants you and your wife to personally report the results of your endeavors to her…"

After a long pause, he continued, "We suspect that whoever killed Dr. Browne will not survive this affair. Oh, and by the way, the queen's private jet aircraft, a BAE 146 RAF ZE 700, and pilot with accompanying crew are waiting for both of you and will be at your disposal until this affair is concluded. We have special scrambled cell phones for both of you and any colleagues you might need in your endeavors. If you require any support of any kind, please press the red button to reach my office at MI5."

Then, Bothwell smiled at Katie and Steve, waved his hand, turned again to the window and the settling mist, relit his pipe, and stared intently at a sparrow hanging desperately to a branch.

7 A DISCOVERY!

The private airplane with an MI5 crew provided by the queen was approaching Leonardo da Vinci-Fiumicino International Airport in Rome when Katie woke up. She had been asleep for a long time or so it seemed. Her head was snuggled onto Steve's lap with his arm wrapped around her waist holding her gently. She was covered with a light weight blue wool blanket and a small pillow cradling her head. As her eyes blinked, Steve bent down and kissed her quietly on her forehead. She stirred and smiled as she looked up into his blue eyes. He was always happy to see her coquettish smile. It was especially for him and no other. After almost five years of marriage, it was like as if they were still on their honeymoon in Straßbourg.

As they started a slow spiral approach to the airport's main landing strip, she mused about what evidence the Vatican Police were going to present. She was already in an analytical mode to assist her husband. She had a special talent to almost read his mind before he even thought of anything. If ever two people were synergistic, they were. It was almost as if they were one person in two different bodies!

When the plane landed and pulled up to a private hangar,

Katie and Steve were met by a Vatican priest who shook their hands and escorted them to a waiting Vatican limousine. The young priest offered some small talk on their transit to the Vatican, but no clue about the conference they were going to attend with the chief inspector general of the Corps of Gendarmerie of Vatican City, Domenico Giani.

The short trip to Vatican City was uneventful, and when Katie and Steve were ushered into the chief inspector's office they were met by an affable smiling balding man with a shaved head wearing wire framed glasses and dressed in a dark blue suit. He was wearing a blue tie with a Windsor knot comfortably knotted under the collar of a white shirt with French cuffs secured by cuff links displaying the familiar Maltese cross of the Sovereign Military Order of Malta which is the pope's branch of that ancient Order. After shaking hands, they were invited to seat themselves in comfortable brown leather chairs arranged in a semicircle in front of his oak desk.

After a brief exchange of pleasantries, the chief inspector got right to the point of their visit, "What was the purpose of your friend, Dr. John Browne's visit to our Secret Archives?"

Steve glanced at Katie and then carefully spoke. "He was hoping to find some record of a visit in 1572 of a Scotsman, David Seton with Pope Gregory XIII."

The chief inspector nodded, "Yes, we found that document on the desk where Dr. Browne was killed by a lead pencil soaked with cyanide. He also had been rendered unconscious with chloroform. We found the broken tip of the lead pencil embedded in his right subclavian vein. His death was almost instantaneous. He didn't suffer."

Steve and Katie drew deep breaths and looked at each other and Steve said, "Thank God!" They were glad of that fact and the inspector's appreciation of their grief for their friend.

"What's this I heard about one of your priests being stabbed with a ceremonial Hanjar dagger?"

The chief inspector took a deep breath and said, "Yes, he was struck down by a Muslim assassin that was a little too quick and didn't finish the job. Fr. Barberini is in guarded condition, but will survive. He has been able to talk and give us some information about his assailant. He has been identified by some fingerprints and DNA left on the handle of the dagger as a person named Aashif al-Fayed, who is a member of the Muslim Brotherhood from Saudi Arabia. We are not quite sure how he was able to become a jihadist mole on our staff at the Vatican Library, but he has been here hidden for a few years. We are now investigating how this happened and checking to see if there are any others of his ilk still lingering in Vatican City."

Steve nodded his head and proffered, "What happened to the briefcase that Dr. Browne had? If he found some evidence he was looking for, it might have been there."

The chief inspector looked directly into Steve's eyes and said firmly, "No, the manuscript he had been looking at was still in place on the desk when we found him and the briefcase contained only a blank notepad and some pencils. Although the manuscript mentions the meeting of David Seton with Pope Gregory, their conversation had more to do with the Hospitaller Order of Saint John on Malta and its surviving the unsuccessful Great Siege of Malta in 1565 by Sultan Suleiman the Magnificent.

"The sultan of the Turkish Ottoman Empire and an overwhelming force of the Ottoman Muslim Turkish Armada, army, and Immortals, with their allies, the Barbary Coast Corsairs, were defeated by the much smaller forces of the Order of Saint John and their allies, the Maltese citizenry. This battle and the later Battle of Lepanto saved Christendom from an invasion and conquest of Europe which was Suleiman's goal. You know the conquest of the world is the overall goal of the Muslim Brotherhood. Much the same as the Nazis."

Steve looked at Katie with an alarmed stare.

Katie turned to the chief inspector and asked, "Is it possible for us to have Dr. Browne's briefcase with its contents? And we would also like to have Dr. Browne's body shipped to Edinburgh if that is possible."

"But of course, we have already made arrangements and

coordinated those efforts with your MI5. We understand that your queen has taken an interest in this matter and we have already taken the proper measures for Dr. Browne's return to his family in Edinburgh. Oh, I also have Dr. Browne's briefcase here and was intending to give it to you, straightaway."

He then leaned down in his chair and came up with Dr. Browne's brown leather briefcase and gave it to Steve.

Steve accepted the well-worn briefcase which was closed and turned it over, thinking how many time he had seen his friend carrying it. He handed it to Katie who promptly opened it and looked inside. Sure enough, there was the closed note pad and the pencils along with a spare handkerchief that Dr. Browne always carried with him. She laid the briefcase in her lap and pulled the notepad out, lifted the cardboard cover, and looked at the white paper with the ruled horizontal light blue lines to keep a writer's script neat. She was about to close the pad when the bright light from the window caught a reflection on the surface of the paper. She lifted the notebook and tuned it slightly and saw more reflections on the page.

Her mind raced at what she saw. There were indentations made by Dr. Browne's pencil as he wrote some notes on those pages. The original had been torn out, but the indentations of his writing were on the blank page in his notebook!

Steve was just finishing speaking with the chief inspector as she put the notebook back into Dr. Browne's briefcase, locked it and placed her hand onto Steve's arm. He glanced at her and saw the glint in her blue eyes—she had found something!

Katie smiled at the chief inspector who finished his remarks and then shook their hands and expressed his best wishes for them, assured them both that his office was glad to assist them in this manner, and expressed his best regards for Dr. Browne's family and the queen.

The young priest that had picked them up at the airport appeared as if by magic and stated that their limousine was waiting and he would be happy to escort them back to the airport. The chief inspector walked with them to the limousine and cheerfully closed the rear door after Katie and Steve entered the vehicle. He waved at them as the limousine sped away toward Leonardo da Vinci International Airport.

8 THE FOG LIFTS

Katie and Steve had just settled into their comfortable seats in the MI5 private jet when a beautiful female, dark haired MI5 agent appeared from a forward compartment of the aircraft and introduced herself. She said her name was Elizabeth Crimmins, but she preferred to be addressed as Betty, and asked if they had eaten while they were in Rome.

"No," Katie volunteered. "We were concentrating on gathering some information while we were at the Vatican and were more interested in the terrorist murder of Dr. Browne than eating, but now that we are back on board the aircraft, I must confess I am hungry. How about you darling?"

Steve had been half listening to the conversation, wondering what Katie had discovered, but now confessed that he was hungry.

"Do you have any snacks on board?" he asked.

Betty laughed, then winked at Katie and said, "You are aware that you are in the hands of the best intelligence officers in the world and we figured that you would be hungry and probably thirsty as well—correct?"

Katie smiled and let her husband confirm Betty's

conclusion.

"Yep, I think we're probably starved to be more accurate," Steve confessed.

The three of them laughed and Betty replied, "We thought so. That's why one of our pilots took the time while you were in the Vatican and went to the Sforno Restaurant and got three pizzas, a tossed salad with olive oil vinaigrette, some Italian craft beer to wash it all down with, and some Neapolitan ice cream with Italian coffee for dessert. Is that okay?"

Steve's eyes opened wider with the mention of each dish and he turned to Katie and said, "I believe we have fallen in with a band of restaurateurs."

Betty laughed and replied, "No, we don't own any restaurants but we know how to find the best."

Betty disappeared forward to the pilot's cabin to inform them that she would be in the galley preparing the meal they had brought from Rome and would serve it as soon as they were airborne and on their way back to Scotland. Another British aircraft was being loaded with Dr. Browne's body as they were taking off.

As they were climbing to altitude, Steve asked Katie, "What did you find that the Vatican Police did not?"

Katie reached down and pulled Dr. Browne's briefcase from beneath her seat and laid it on her lap. She opened it up, pulled out his notebook, and handed it to her husband. "Take a look at the first page."

Steve flipped the cardboard cover up and glanced at the first page—it was empty and he looked quizzically at Katie.

She looked at Steve and said, "See, that's what they did. They just glanced at the blank paper without seeing the indentations on the paper that John's pencil made as he was writing. That's the mistake they and John's assassin both made. They forgot that when you write with a pencil, indentations are made on the paper underneath unless you put cardboard between the pages. Turn the page obliquely so the light emphasizes the indentations—see, there's something there. And look at the drawing of a symbol on the bottom of the page, as if John wanted to emphasize it. He pressed harder to make the drawing darker and then drew a lighter circle around it. What do you make of it, honey?"

Steve was amazed—she was correct. He had just glanced at it, not noting the indentations made by writing by hand with a pencil. Most people today used an electronic device with a keyboard to write or use voice recognition to write by dictation. They are not acquainted with the old fashioned ways of writing.

Steve looked intently at the indentations and the drawing at the bottom of the page. He said to Katie, "You know, it looks like a chevron with a small circle just under the point of the chevron. Just like the one on the brass handle of the circular stone door in the floor of Saint Mary Chapel."

"I thought the same thing. I know I've seen that symbol someplace before, but where? Steve, I've got it! Isn't that somewhere in the symbols used by the Knights Templar and the Fréres Maçons? You know, like the hooked X in the runes of the Swedish Cistercians? You know that the popes had wanted to join the Order of Saint John with the Knights Templar so they could control their enterprises and wealth. Maybe that was why the manuscript John was looking at described their conversation about the Order of Saint John and Malta."

Steve opined, "Could be, but David and his fellow Templar knights were upset about the treachery they believed happened with the Sandilands affair. David Seton was Catholic and the Protestants were taking over Scotland and Ireland just as they had done under Henry VIII and his daughter Queen Elizabeth I in England. There was a struggle for control of the monarchies and the wealth of nations, and the pope had even excommunicated Queen Elizabeth and declared that she was not the lawful queen of England, which was why Mary, Queen of Scots, had to be eliminated."

Katie added, "Yes, but this was in 1572 while Mary was still alive and held prisoner by the English. She wasn't executed until February 8, 1587."

Steve said, "You're absolutely right. But whatever John found, he was on the right track."

About that time, Betty and James, one of the pilots, appeared with the pizza and beer, laid the meal out on the small table in the dining area of the private plane, and motioned for Katie and Steve to join them. As they sat down, Betty introduced James and as they shook hands, James told them that his fellow pilot Henry, or Hank as he called him, would join them later after he finished eating his share of the meal, and then he would trade places with Hank.

They had all finished eating and Betty had stored away all of the plates, silverware, glasses in the galley, when they passed over the white cliffs of Dover.

Betty, who was English, leaned over and stared out the window. She muttered quietly, almost reverently to Katie and Steve, "I always get a chill when I see those cliffs. You know the cliffs can be seen by binoculars from France. Hitler, when he was planning for invasion, was caught on camera looking longingly at those white shimmering cliffs unattainable in the distance. It's too bad that an unseen enemy of Britain has breached those walls by innocent enough immigration"

Then she turned, leaving Steve and Katie to ponder what she had said, almost without thinking and as an unaware spoken thought.

The evening was fast darkening and the stars were beginning to come out when their plane touched down at Edinburgh International Airport located approximately five miles west of downtown Edinburgh, just off M8 and M9 highway and between Edinburgh and Glasgow.

9 MACINTOSH MANOR

The page from Dr. Browne's notebook had been fully photographed, and a soft dusting of graphite powder applied to the indentations of his writing had revealed what he had scribbled onto the pad just before he was killed. Fortunately, they probably didn't make any more sense to the Muslim Brotherhood than they did at first glance to Katie and Steve. However, they were certain they were on the correct path when they postulated that someone familiar with Templar and Fréres Maçon symbols would understand it.

The notes Dr. Browne had written started with one line containing the words, "Ratisbon tombstones, Dom Saint Peter," and underneath that the phrase, "as it is above, so it is below," followed by, "the Sword of Schönfeld points the way in the Chapel of the English? Or the Germans?" followed by the phrase, "the skull is where bones are interred."

It appeared that it was written in haste without any sentence structure and was only words he intended to jog his memory about what he had learned from the ancient manuscript relating to the conversation David Seton had with the pope.

As Steve was mulling over the enigmatic notes in his office, Katie walked through the door of his office and announced

45

that she had just received a telephone call from Carolyn Rood that she and Christopher were coming to Scotland in three weeks for the celebration of the completion of their new manor house. They also offered their condolences over the death of Dr. Browne. She said that their lawyer, Diamond Dave, and his wife Debbie were coming with them since he had negotiated the sale of the fifty acres of land and contracted the building of the house for them at Loch Moy, the homeland of the MacIntoshes. They were naming their house MacIntosh Manor.

Katie said that she had already cleared his schedule and checked with Natalie who said that she would see if Dietrich could get a leave of absence from his duties in the Luftwaffe for that week. She would be bringing Kira Ann since she would be terribly hurt if she couldn't see her favorite cousins.

She said she was still trying to track down Dr. Fox, but his office said that he was "out of pocket" with a group of graduate students at a dig outside Veracruz, Mexico, where Cortez had scuttled his ships, but he would be checking in this weekend. She would clear his calendar so he could come to Scotland for that week.

Steve gazed admiringly at his wife, thinking how fortunate he was to be her husband and have her as his private secretary. He marveled at her organizational skills. He inwardly felt that he was her Dr. Watson.

The three weeks passed quickly and suddenly everyone had arrived in Scotland. Carolyn and Christopher with Diamond Dave and his wife had arrived three days earlier and had already left for Loch Moy. Carolyn wanted to open up the house and get the guest bedrooms ready for everyone. And besides, she wanted to get some surprises for Kira Ann and fix up a special room just for her. Dietrich was able to get a month's leave of absence since his recent promotion to full colonel.

Natalie had been contacted by her nursing friend, Rania, and her new husband, Anton Svoboda. Rania was anxious for everyone to meet the love of her life who had protected her from her brother, Ahmed, and father, Mohammad, who had tried to kill her for loving a Czech Christian. She had reminded them both that her mother was Christian and had been sold into slavery to her father.

She saw her mother killed by a sniper's bullet in Sarajevo during the Baltic War and did not want to be part of a jihadist world. That was why she had run away and was protected by Anton and his family.

She wanted to be part of the Muslim Reformist movement started in the United States by Dr. M. Zuhdi Jasser. She had read his book, *A Battle for the Soul of Islam*, and was greatly impressed by his desire to bring Islam into the twenty-first century and eliminate Wahhabi Sharia Law and all jihadist elements in Islam. She felt his organization, the American Islamic Forum for Democracy, was the answer for all modern Muslims interested in peace on earth and tolerance among all religions. She called him the Martin Luther of Islam.

Everyone had showed up in Edinburgh. Natalie and Dietrich with Kira Ann and her "Auntie" Rania and "Uncle" Anton in tow, who were also staying at the Balmoral Hotel. Dr. Randall Fox, who had typically showed up at the last minute, was also staying in the hotel. The Balmoral Hotel was where Natalie and Dietrich had been spending their honeymoon when all of their subsequent adventures began with the near death of her husband at the hands of an insane Muslim Brotherhood assassin—Rania's father Mohammad!

Steve along with Katie, Natalie, Dietrich, and Kira Ann squeezed into Steve's silver Jaguar sedan with Rania and Anton going in Randall's rented Mercedes C class sedan. Randall was comfortable driving in the United Kingdom because of his many digs there, and besides he wanted to show off his driving skills to Natalie's friends. The distance from Edinburgh to Loch Moy in Inverness is approximately 155 miles and would be a nice drive to the Highlands.

When they all arrived at Loch Moy, they drove up the long winding road to MacIntosh Manor. Carolyn and Christopher, along with Diamond Dave and Debbie, were standing on the concrete walkway outside the entrance stairs waiting for the two cars to stop on the bricked circular driveway in front of the entrance.

It was a typical large traditional Scottish manor that was made of limestone and granite. The main house was three stories tall with a hexagonal tower having four alternating windows to the right of its main entrance. The tower housed an all glassed-in elevator that provided its passengers an excellent view of the grounds as it ascended. There was a two-story wing off the side of the main house containing six large apartment-sized bedrooms and two smaller-sized regular bedrooms suitable for young children—one on each floor.

The lower floor of the main house had a marble-floored foyer inside the front entrance which echoed when anyone walked across it to the entrance room. A long winding staircase to the second floor that contained what could have been a ballroom but was actually a conference room with walnut paneling on three sides and one mirrored wall that made it look even larger. There were hallways that surrounded the main room which led to several smaller decorated rooms containing a private office, library with a reading area next to a window, a music room with a grand piano, a hobby room, and a photography and painting studio with a small gallery off to the side to exhibit Christopher's collections of art and photographs.

The entire front of this floor was a wide oak parquet hallway with three double windows that were from floor to ceiling. An alcove with a window looking toward the side of the house was nestled between the tower and a single window peering out toward the front from the music room on the right corner of the house.

The entire third floor upstairs was the master bedroom with a gigantic bed that their large grey cat, Balthazar, was determined to rule. There were walnut cabinets, dressers and lighted makeup table, a corner desk with library shelves and books on either side, double clothes closets with adjoining private dressing rooms, sauna, bath with walk in showers, and a sunken Jacuzzi hot tub close to one of the windows looking forward onto the entrance grounds. Down the hall was an exercise room that Carolyn and Christopher used early each morning.

The lower floor contained a maid's quarters and a butler's quarters, which Carolyn only had for occasional use if needed, and a large walnut-paneled great room with a statue of a knight in sixteenth century armor with a large Crusader's sword standing to one side of the large walnut double doors guarding the entrance. Inside the great room was another library with a large limestone fireplace with screen and gas logs in the middle of a paneled wall. There was a fully stocked walnut bar with stools next to it. At the far side of the room was a large flat panel television with a surround sound system. Part of the library contained a collection of DVDs and CDs.

There was also a large sectional leather couch with accompanying leather chairs. Down the hall outside of the great room was a large dining room with a walnut table capable of seating sixteen people. Next to the dining room was a large kitchen with a breakfast nook off to the side.

Outside the house was a detached six-car garage with electronic doors, and behind the garage were two tennis courts and a large swimming pool with a hot tub Jacuzzi. There was also a gazebo in the middle of a large formal garden with willow trees overlooking the loch.

As they all exited their cars, Kira Ann ran up to her cousin Carolyn, wrapped her arms around Carolyn's, waist and looked up at her smiling.

"Do you have any Neapolitan ice cream?"

Natalie was horrified and walked over to her daughter and admonished her, "Don't you think you should say hello first and then introduce your "Auntie" Rania and "Uncle" Anton before you ask for some ice cream?"

Kira looked down and then up at Carolyn and Christopher with her lower lip pouting out, she said, "I'm sorry, it's just that I've been waiting soooo long for some ice cream!"

She had stretched her hands out as she said soooo, and it completely melted Carolyn's and Christopher's heart. Then

Kira introduced Rania and Anton to Carolyn and Christopher and their guests, Debbie and Diamond Dave, after Debbie whispered into her ear what their names were.

Randall leaned over to Dietrich and whispered, "They start young, don't they?"

Dietrich smiled and then chuckled, "I know what's happening, but I still love it—she is so cute, just like her mother."

Carolyn took Kira's hand and led her into the house toward the kitchen. Everyone else smiled at each other and followed along into the manor with bags in hand.

10 RANIA'S STORY

Carolyn had led the way for everyone to get a Cook's tour of the main house while Christopher and Diamond Dave took their luggage to each of the new arrival's suites in the south wing of the main house. Christopher had carefully sorted out everyone's luggage before they had entered the main entrance to follow Carolyn on their tour. After Diamond had finished their task, they joined their wives and helped escort everyone through all of the rooms of their newly finished manor house. After the tour and answering all of the questions their guests had concerning the estate, the details of the manor house's construction and all of the various vignettes concerning different phases of construction and any difficulties encountered that were common in any building of a dream house, Carolyn and Christopher led everyone to the main floor and the Great Room past the guarding knight in shining armor.

Kira seemed to be fascinated with any problems a knight might have getting in and out of such a heavy suit of armor. She had many questions that her doting father lovingly answered in great detail. She seemed happy and satisfied with his explanations and then wandered over to Christopher who

51

was engaged in a conversation with Katie and Steve about their visit at the Vatican. Katie, Steve and Carolyn were sitting on a large brown leather couch to the side of the massive fireplace and Christopher had pulled his leather side chair close to them. Rania and her husband, Anton, were seated next to Debbie and Diamond on another matching couch opposite Katie, Steve and Carolyn.

Randall was seated at the bar when Natalie and Dietrich joined him. He had just poured some single malt Lismore scotch— neat of course—into a tumbler with a side glass of soda. He looked up at them, then asked them if they wanted the same. They nodded their approval of the invitation and he obediently complied.

Kira smiled bravely, tugged on Christopher's sleeve and asked, "May I have some ice cream—please?"

Christopher looked at her and then at Natalie, who had been observing her daughter despite the conversation with Randall and her husband, Dietrich. She winked at Christopher and nodded her approval. Christopher excused himself, got up from his chair, and holding Kira's hand, led her into the kitchen for her long awaited ice cream.

Rania was feeling a little tired, excused herself, and said she was going to the library and look at the books to see if there was one she could find to read that might ease her tiredness. She felt she needed a little quiet and the library on the second floor just might do the trick. As she took the glassed-in elevator to the second floor, her mind started to wander back to her childhood when her father would not allow her to read certain books and her mother would sneak books into her room for her.

Her mother was raised as a Christian and, even though she was a virtual slave to her husband, she was determined that her daughter was going to be able to read many different books and later get a comprehensive education just like she had before she had been kidnapped as a teenager in college and sold to her husband as a slave. She had been a student in Dresden, Germany, when she was abducted and taken to a private slave market in Sarajevo and sold to the highest bidder.

Rania never forgot her mother's desire for her to escape her bondage and live her own life freely and follow her dreams of being a nurse. Rania had been lucky to get her public education in Sarajevo just like her half-brother, Ahmed. Her mother was so happy when Rania told her that she had received a full scholarship to Karlova University Nursing School at the Karlova Medical Center in Prague, Czech Republic. Maybe she could escape her father's clutches.

Rania, who resembled the actress Audrey Hepburn, had met Natalie during their first year as students at Karlova and they had been roommates and studied together and became best friends.

It had been the Christmas season of 1990 while Rania was in middle school in Sarajevo during the last years of the Balkan Wars that she saw her mother shot down and killed by a sniper's bullet as she was crossing a street with a Christmas gift she had just bought to give to her daughter. It was a necklace with a golden Ankh—the ancient Egyptian symbol of life that she wanted her daughter to have in the pursuit of her future career as a nurse saving lives.

She remembered her mother's last wish for her as she lay dying in the hospital when she looked up at her, pressed her gift into her daughter's hands and whispered, "For you my darling, to remind you to save lives, not take them. I love you!" And then she died with a smile on her face and tears in her eyes.

Rania suddenly broke the trance of her remembrances and realized that she had already absent-mindedly left the elevator, entered the library, and was standing in front of a row of books of poetry staring at a copy of Kahlil Gibran's book, *A Tear and a Smile.*

She had read the book when she was in high school and had liked it then. She took the book from the shelf and casually flipped through it until she came to the story, "A Smile and a Tear."

She read it and then thought to herself, "How can I express

simply that I choose to follow the light of wisdom espoused by Dr. M. Zuhdi Jasser and his international appeal for an Islamic Reformation rather that the present sword of theocracy and jihad leading to the revenge that killed my innocent mother?"

She wrinkled her brow and smiled when she thought about the word, wisdom. She remembered what Albert Einstein had said about genius. He commented about genius when asked as a professor at Princeton University how he would define it.

He replied, "Genius is the ability to take something complicated and make it simple."

She recalled reading about the ancient Egyptian pharaoh Akhenaten, husband of Nefertiti and Tut's father who lived 1300 years before Christ, and how he had cast out the panoply of gods in favor of one, Ra, the Sun God, as the giver of life and the architect of the universe. The Ankh was the symbol of that life force.

She instinctively moved her right hand to the golden Ankh on the gold necklace around her neck that her mother had given her with her last breath of life. She had passed this gift of life to her to remember when she, as a nurse, would follow Allah's and her mother's Christian God's admonition to save life and not take it.

As she thought about her mother, tears began to well up in her eyes and began to flow down her cheeks. She took a handkerchief from her purse and wiped the tears from her eyes.

She mused about the Ankh, this symbol of life.

Moses would later stop the Hebrews' worship of the golden calf and many gods by bringing down from the Mountain of Sinai the Ten Commandments from God and led them to the Promised Land.

Later a young Jew name Jesus, who spent part of his childhood safely in Egypt after his parents had fled there to avoid Herod's wrath, would simplify those Ten Commandments into one Golden Rule and a simple prayer to the Lord God during his Sermon on the Mount.

She reflected further about how the archangel Gabriel in 610 CE revealed to Muhammad the first verse of the Koran and later revelations from the Lord God Allah as revealed in the Holy Book of the Koran meant to enlighten the world.

Her thoughts then wandered to the first time she heard Dr. M. Zuhdi Jasser's iTunes podcast app—*Reform This*. It was then she became aware of his Islamic Reform Movement to bring Islam into the modern world and take its place as a peaceful pillar of the monotheistic tradition without theocratic rule. She thought, "He believes in the principles of universal individual freedom and liberty with separation of church and state."

She read his book, *A Battle for the Soul of Islam*, and became a follower of his organization, the American Islamic Forum for Democracy. In her heart she felt he is the voice of every reasonable modern man and woman of Islamic faith. She had heard him compared with the courage of Martin Luther when he challenged the theocracy of the Roman Catholic Church with the posting of his Ninety-Five Theses of 1517 which began the Protestant Reformation.

As a modern woman of Islamic faith she felt his American Islamic Forum for Democracy and his book describing his journey to reform Islam is important for the whole world order and a lasting peace in the clash between the world's three major monotheistic religions which are the three pillars of the one God envisioned so long ago in Egypt by the Pharaoh Akhenaten and his wife Nefertiti.

All of a sudden, she was shaken back into consciousness by Kira Ann's little hand tugging on her dress. She looked down upon Kira's beaming face and smiled.

"Auntie Rania, could you help me get a book off a shelf? I can't reach it!"

Rania reached down and picked Kira up, thinking of how much Kira reminded her of herself when she was a child and longed to read books, but was forbidden by her father to read certain books. She fondly remembered when her mother would secretly get many essential books, especially history books, for her to read. Her mother felt that to be a free and equal woman, reading many books was a must.

She kissed Kira on the cheek and carried her to the library shelves where Kira eagerly pointed to the book she wanted to read. It was one of the classics, *Winnie the Pooh*, written by English author A. A. Milne in 1926.

Kira carefully removed the book from its resting place on the shelf and held it close to her chest. Her eyes brightened and she said, "Thank you, Auntie Rania."

Rania lowered her to the floor and she ran over to a comfortable burgundy leather chair in an alcove next to a window and began reading.

A tear slipped from Rania's eye and slid down her cheek. A tear and a smile!

11 WHAT NOW?

Everyone was now up from a restful sleep and gathered in the dining room on the first floor where breakfast was being served by a temporary staff from a local restaurant that Carolyn and Christopher had hired for the communion of friends who had gathered at MacIntosh Manor to participate in the *Grail Quest* of which they were all now a part.

Carolyn had decided that a traditional Texas breakfast of scrambled eggs with grits, a choice of bacon and sausage, hashed brown potatoes, salsa sauce, mixed fruit, orange juice or grapefruit juice, coffee and cream, and of course, local spring water. It was just what the doctor ordered!

After everyone had finished their meal and Kira was taken by Maura, one of the trusted ladies on her staff for the duration, to the library to finish her reading of the Pooh books, Christopher invited everyone into the conference room on the second floor.

As they entered, they could see that the large walnut conference table had a note pad with a ballpoint pen, a napkin, a small goblet with Christopher's coat of arms emblazoned on it, and a small glass dish with the Rood crest on it situated at a spot for everyone at the table. There were two large bowls of assorted nuts and three bowls of assorted jelly beans. Just like President Reagan, Christopher liked everyone to be comfortable during any serious discussions. Christopher sat at the head of the table while Carolyn sat at the opposite end in the Scottish fashion. Everyone else sat where they chose. There were no place cards.

Christopher took charge of the meeting and opened it by saying, "Steve, I understand that you and Katie have some good news and some bad news for us and I understand also that Rania and Anton have something to tell us about this affair."

The two couples nodded their heads in agreement and Steve deferred to Rania and her husband to fill in the details of their news.

Rania looked at her husband and then at her friends, Natalie and Dietrich, and said, "First let me say how sorry Anton and I are to learn of your friend, Dr. Browne's death. My husband and I had heard rumors about something going to happen in the Vatican while we were visiting the mosque a few weeks ago in Prague. There was idle chatter among some of the men that the Muslim Brotherhood was involved in stopping a problem from an enemy who had killed two of their brothers five years ago.

"I eavesdropped on their conversation, which I don't believe they thought I understood. They were speaking in a Bosnian dialect that I happen to know. They probably thought I only understood the Prague dialect of Czech and the Arabic language. I also happen to speak and write six other languages.

"They were whispering about a grail and a skull that a Dr. Browne from Edinburgh was looking for, and in the conversation Natalie's and Dietrich's names came up. Then I heard the name of the two members of the Brotherhood who had been killed and I realized they were talking about my father and half-brother! I gasped when they mentioned their names, but I don't believe they heard me.

"They furthered mentioned that at a bar in Edinburgh one

night, one of the graduate students at Edinburgh University who was helping Dr. Fox and Dr. Browne had bragged about how he was part of a real search for the Holy Grail and some kind of a skull. He was overheard by an undergraduate Palestinian student bartender who was a member of the Brotherhood. That student apparently relayed the conversation to the Brotherhood in Saudi Arabia where they said they would take care of Dr. Browne. The Brotherhood has a long memory."

There were looks of amazement around the table, but then Steve Grant broke the silence, "Everyone should understand that the entire Western World has been infiltrated by a silent army of Islamic terrorists and sympathizers. They are everywhere and growing in number.

"Some are moles waiting for an opportunity to be activated. Some are active recruiters of native Western-born Muslims, and others are active terrorists who are bomb-makers and developers of methods to spread terror by the destruction of Western infrastructure such as burning vital interstate highway bridges, damaging water supplies in metro areas, disrupting air and land travel, damaging dams, blowing up buildings, running down pedestrians, street killings and beheadings, shooting or blowing up innocent civilians at sporting events, theaters, nightclubs, schools, civic gatherings, and public demonstrations.

"Their intent is general unrest, disruption and confusion. They have been quietly over the last few decades since World War II laying the seeds of division in some parts of the Western world with the grouping of people into classes of nationalities, sexes, races, creeds, cultures, and religions. The old Roman concept of divide and conquer. Instead of bringing people together as individuals following a course of freedom and individual liberty without theocratic control or dictatorship of the elite, they are following the little red playbook of Mao.

"They are branding people as crusaders, religious zealots, racists, fascists, sexists, misogynists, or any other evil in order to confuse the issue and lead to unrest, demonstrations, and anarchy. It's a new brand of guerrilla warfare involving the civilian population instead of organized armies, navies, or air forces. Their intent is to undermine a nation's ideals and will. It's unique because you don't know where or who the enemy is.

"Starting with a nation's educational system, and their own freedoms and liberal laws, they have been brainwashing children in the Middle and Far East and many isolated areas of Western nations just like Hitler did with the Hitler Youth. Instead of teaching children to evaluate issues with reason and consideration on both sides of a question and then making an individual decision, they are following a doctrine of rule of the masses with all following in lockstep to the rule of a small elite—just like sheep being led by a Judas goat to the slaughter. It's like taking a snake into your tent. They want Sharia Law to replace a nation's own laws, so their imams with the bidding of their masters can control the masses.

"That is why border security and knowing your enemy is so important. And they are also active in cybercrime—hacking, ransomware and identification fraud.

"Some of their allied organizations are involved in kidnapping for sex trafficking, organ transplants in hospitals around the world, and slave marketing throughout the world using ruses of all sorts."

Steve's words caused everyone's jaws to drop. Everyone had bewildered looks on their faces and questions in their eyes.

And Steve looked around and said, "And that's just for openers."

Christopher took a drink of water and cleared his throat and then asked, "Do you and Katie know what happened to Dr. Browne and what he might have discovered at the Vatican?"

Katie lifted her hand and replied, "We have deciphered Dr. Browne's notes, But unfortunately the murderer, a priest named Marco Baronio, who was a Brotherhood mole at the Vatican whose real name is Aashif al-Fayed from Saudi Arabia, got away with Dr. Browne's original note, but the indentations made from Dr. Browne's pencil on the paper underneath the note allowed us to lift his writing off that page.

"Marco Baronio had been on the Vatican staff for a few years and no one suspected who he really was. He was hasty in his attempted murder of a priest, Roberto Barberini, who was a little tougher than the assassin thought. He hurried the job and the priest survived. Vatican photographs, DNA, and fingerprint analysis were key in the identification of the false priest. We assume he is back behind the Crescent Curtain in Saudi Arabia.

"Dr. Browne's note was short, but contained the drawing of a chevron with a small circle under the point of the chevron."

Randall suddenly lifted his head from his two clasped hands that was supporting his chin and blurted, "The very same emblem at the bottom of David Seton's letter and the brass handle on the stone door at the chapel! John must have seen it on the Vatican manuscript and placed some significance of it in what he wrote. What followed the drawing on his note?"

Randall saw the impatient look in Katie's eyes and timidly said, "Sorry for the interruption."

Katie smiled and continued, "As I was about to say, under the drawing were four sentences—kind of. The sentences were, 'Ratisbon tombstones' and under that, 'Dom Saint Peter,' followed by 'As it is above, so it is below.' Then that is followed by the phrase, 'The Sword of Schönfeld points the way in the Chapel of the English? Or the Germans?' The last entry sentence is, 'The skull is where the bones are interred.'

"I'm sure this has something to do with Templar symbolism and I doubt if too many members of the Muslim Brotherhood would understand it. That may be good news, but I suspect that we all may be targeted for observation to see where we go. They must be interested in the possibility that there might be a Holy Grail they could steal and exploit, and in the process kill a few infidels—us!"

With that statement, everyone blinked and swallowed hard.

Randall said, "I think I know what John was getting at. The symbol of the chevron and circle is the constant—the breadcrumbs being dropped on the trail of the grail. It means, 'follow the breadcrumbs.' I don't know exactly what the symbol is, but I'll bet it has some significance related to the skull or the grail or both!

"The sentence, 'Ratisbon tombstones, Dom Saint Peter,' probably refers to the Saint Peter Cathedral in Regensburg in Bavaria, Germany. Dom is 'cathedral' in German."

"Wait a minute," said Dietrich, "I thought the note said Ratisbon?"

Randall answered, "It does, but the modern name is Regensburg. Ratisbon is the ancient name for the city, and the tombstones are probably in the church graveyard or maybe inside the cathedral, and I'll bet that's where David Seton and his wife are buried. The Seton Archives state that David Seton left Scotland with some of his fellow Templar Knights in 1572 and that David took his family and wife. His fellow Templars probably left as well since they were the Frére Maçon hiding out with the Hospitallers and seeking refuge with fellow Catholic Hospitallers in Bavaria. Bavaria is primarily Catholic and not Lutheran like the rest of Germany."

Christopher entered the conversation and added, "As it is above, so it is below refers to heaven and earth. It has something to do with Jesus and the grail!"

No one could figure out the third sentence, but Randall said he believed it meant ossuary because that is a container for bones and that somehow Schönfeld's sword is involved, but where is the grail? And what does the question marks associated with chapel of the English and chapel of the Germans mean?

Natalie had been listening with great interest to the dialogue and remarked, "If we are trying to find the trail of David Seton and what he has done with the Holy Grail and the skull of John the Baptist, why don't we let Dietrich and me go with Rania and Anton to Bavaria to see if he and his wife are buried there, and maybe there are more clues we can find in or around the cathedral or the cemetery around the cathedral?"

Randall looked up thoughtfully and said, "Why do we

believe the skull is John the Baptist? You know that the original patron of the Hospitallers was John the Apostle or maybe even Saint John of Patmos, the writer of the Book of Revelation. We are not really sure. It is interesting that both the Templars and the Hospitallers had John the Baptist as their patron saint."

Natalie had been listening to all of the discussion and said, "Professor, why couldn't the skull be Saint Mary of Magdalene? After all, the Chapel of Saint Mary at the thirteen sycamores was dedicated to her. The Orders of the Templars and later the Temple Malta—the Frére Maçon—frequently consecrated chapels and cathedrals in her name. Isn't that the heretical Cathar and Gnostic origin of the Sacred Feminine and the eclipse of Venus that occurs every two hundred years? Isn't that the reason for the Venus or rose window in all of their chapels and cathedrals? Isn't it, that eclipse that led us to the discovery of the secret room beneath the Saint Mary Chapel at Mount Lothian that began our quest?"

Randall exclaimed, "You know, you're correct, it could be! We should be able to tell if the skull is intact whether it is a male or female skull."

Diamond Dave and his wife Debbie had been quietly watching the conversations and Diamond leaned forward and remarked, "You know this is very interesting. It is just how a bunch of lawyers would sit around a conference table and try to figure out how to get their client off the hook!"

Debbie tried to muffle her laughter at her husband's remark and countered, "That's just like David. He's just like Rhett Butler in the book *Gone with the Wind* trying to break the Union blockade of Georgia.

With that, Christopher rose and looked down the table at Carolyn and before he could say anything, she said, "How about we take a break, have some lunch and afterward take a stroll in our new garden and let some of this discussion settle a little before we make any decisions?"

Everyone stood up and stretched their arms when Kira Ann entered the room with her companion and reported, "We're hungry!" as she looked up at Maura and added, "Aren't we?"

12 THE PLAN

The formal garden was beautiful with fine gravel pathways and small gardens of lovely flowers in a mosaic design that resembled from overhead a kaleidoscope of color. Carolyn, with the help of Debbie, Natalie, Katie and Rania, had laid out the tables for lunch and a smorgasbord luncheon buffet was spread by her staff. There was a variety of foods and dishes such as hors d'oeuvres, hot and cold ham and beef, traditional Scottish Haggis, smoked and pickled salmon, various cheeses, deviled eggs, salads with relishes, and of course beer, red and white wine, and single malt, highland whiskies for the bold of heart. There was even cold spring water to wash it all down. The desert was chocolate covered strawberries and Neapolitan ice cream—Kira's favorite!

After lunch, everyone had an opportunity to stroll through the gardens in friendly conversation with everyone getting to know Rania and Anton a little bit better. Carolyn and Kira Ann were sitting on the edge of a small arched bridge over the small stream meandering through the gardens. They were looking at some of the large goldfish swimming lazily in the warm sunlight filtering through the crystal clear water. Carolyn was busily answering the myriad of questions her cousin was asking, when she looked at her watch and suddenly realized that the schedule of events planned for the day was inexorably slipping away.

She stood up and picked up Kira and walked toward her guests who were discussing details of the morning meeting. Carolyn turned Kira over to Maura and asked her if she would show Kira some of the paintings and sculptures in their house before putting her in her bed for her afternoon nap. Kira looked up at her cousin and then her mother Natalie, who nodded her approval of the suggestion.

Kira started to voice her disapproval of taking a nap when she noticed her mother's facial expression known only to mothers and daughters that she was indeed going to be taking a nap. Kira held her head down a little and uttered, "Yes, ma'am," and followed along with Maura, holding her hand as they disappeared into the house.

Christopher took the hint and announced that they needed to reconvene in the conference room and make some decisions as to their next course of action.

After everyone had a chance to freshen up in their rooms for a few minutes, they all met together in the conference room and took their seats to see what action they should take.

Christopher turned toward Randall and said, "Professor, what do you make of the situation that we have? How should we proceed?"

Randall looked at his friends and said, "As you all know from this morning's discussions, the logical thing to do is to take Dr. Browne's clues and follow them. I believe there is some danger and I would suggest that we take advantage of Sir Richard Bothwell's suggestions and have scrambled cell phones assigned to each of us with the fingerprint security devices and coded numbers so we all can be in secure contact at all times. Oh, Steve, will the queen's private jet still be available to us as we sort out this mystery?"

"Yes, I believe so," replied Steve. "The airplane and MI5 crew are at our disposal, or for that matter, any other means of conveyance deemed necessary. Sir Richard has promised the queen that Dr. Browne's death would not be in vain and that our national treasure would be retrieved."

"Okay, then it seems obvious to me that the next step should be going to Regensburg to find the grave sites of David Seton and his wife, Marjory of Blackhall. Who do all of you think should get this assignment?"

Unanimous voices said, "You!"

Randall smiled and said, "Well, thank you all, I was planning to include myself, but I think it would be wise to have Natalie and Dietrich along with Rania and Anton. Would that be good for everyone?"

Christopher raised his hand and said, "I want to go too, if that wouldn't crowd the scene."

Carolyn chided her husband and said, "Not so fast, you have guests and I think Kira should stay here with us so as to look perfectly normal if we are being shadowed. Kira and I would be greatly disappointed if you weren't here. She has been looking forward to spending some time with us, isn't that so, Natalie?"

Natalie and Dietrich had to admit that was the case.

"I don't want to take any chances and we need your help to make sure we are all protected, even though we have ample electronic security here at the manor. Katie and Steve can monitor everything going on through their contacts with MI5 if they want to stay here with us."

Carolyn looked at Katie and Steve and said, "Is that possible, Steve?"

Steve looked at Katie and she nodded her approval and he replied, "Yes, we have been given full authority by Sir Richard. If you don't mind, we can make your manor our command center for the duration. I'll see if I can get the queen's MI5 jet and crew moved to Inverness Airport at Dalcross. It is only about 14 miles from here and is a private airport where we can provide security from all prying eyes. The MI5 staff will be thrilled to be in Inverness."

"See Christopher, you can be involved electronically with

the expedition to Regensburg without leaving the comfort of our house."

Christopher smiled, but inwardly, he really wanted to go. He had acquiesced reluctantly because he knew Carolyn was right.

"Okay, it's settled then," replied Randall. "The five of us will go to Regensburg with the MI5 people and the queen's jet. Is everyone agreed?"

Everyone breathed a sigh of relief at the decision.

Anton smiled at his wife and said, "I'm with you darling, always," as they looked lovingly at each other, glad to be reunited with their friends Natalie and Dietrich for this opportunity to share in their grail quest and adventure.

Rania and Natalie had no idea how fortunate this decision would be.

13 REGENSBURG

The necessary changes had been made. MI5 had moved the queen's jet airplane to the Inverness Airport and the crew to Inverness and a military security team to the airport. One of the staff, Betty, had been moved into one of the guest rooms at MacIntosh Manor, and other MI5 staff had set up an electronic command post with a large, flat-screen ultrahigh definition television monitor with accompanying communication gear and desks in the manor's conference room. This setup was capable of multiple satellite visual and audio surveillance and communication anywhere in the world.

James Stewart and Henry "Hank" MacFarland, Betty's copilots, were staying at the Inverness Palace Hotel, ready to take the team of five at a moment's notice to wherever they needed to go. Elizabeth "Betty" Crimmins was the SAS team commander specially assigned to the queen's jet airplane when Dr. Browne had been murdered. Sir Richard had specifically assigned her as commander and her other team members to this detail because of their ability not only to fly any kind of aircraft but their linguistic skills and training as Special Air Service (SAS) agents fully trained in all military skills.

They hid their abilities and no one would suspect who they

really were, and that was the way they liked it. They hid in the shadows with no one suspecting how deadly they could be—a formidable foe in any tough situation.

Betty had already coordinated and tested all of the electronic equipment and scrambled cell phones that had been issued to all of the members of the research team who were part of the effort to recover the artifacts that had been taken from Saint Mary Chapel and spirited out of the United Kingdom by David Seton and his fellow Knights Templar in 1572. Dr. Randall Fox would lead the team of five to Regensburg, Bavaria, in Germany.

The Saint Peter Cathedral in Regensburg is the most important example of Gothic architecture in Bavaria and is located northeast of Munich. In 739, Saint Boniface chose the area for the church to be built, which was located at the north gate of an old Roman fort. The cathedral was rebuilt in the High Gothic style in 1273. In 1385-1415 the elaborate main entrance to the west was completed. The rest of the new edifice and cloister was completed by 1538. In 1828-1841 King Ludwig I completed a neo Gothic restoration, and the towers and spires were built in 1859-1869. About 600 years were consumed in its construction. The cathedral is considered to be the most significant Gothic cathedral in southern Germany. In the western part of the central nave is a bronze memorial for Prince-Bishop Cardinal Philipp Wilhelm.

The cathedral is located in the heart of the city at Saint Peter Domplatz, just a couple of blocks from the southern branch of the Danube River. The Domplatz Straße, Krautermarkt, Niedermunstergasse, and the Unter dem Schwibbögen circle the cathedral and its associated buildings. It is next to a complex of buildings, the Museum Saint Ulrich to the east, the Domschatz museum close by and directly north of the cathedral, and the Porta Praetoria to the north of the Domschatz museum. The Krautermarkt and the Domplatz Straße are close to the cathedral on the west and south bordering the church grounds.

After researching all of the hotels near the cathedral, Dr.

Fox chose the Hotel Bischhofshof Am Dom at Krautermarkt right across the street from Saint Peter Cathedral. It is a five-star hotel with an outside and several inside restaurants that are very quaint with excellent menus. The rooms are large and excellent with all of the amenities.

There was a private airport nearby, the EDNR or Regensburg Oberhub Airport, which was fourteen miles to the northwest of the city center which could accommodate the queen's jet with full service and have sufficient security from the Bundesnachtrichtendienst or the Federal Intelligence service, directly subordinated to the chancellor's office in Berlin. They could also solicit the aid of the Bundespolizei which is the uniformed federal police force in Germany that would provide cover for their investigation of the Saint Peter Cathedral's interior and exterior.

Randall provided the information he had obtained, including the name of the Regensburg Oberhub Airport to Katie and Steve, not realizing that they and Betty had already determined from their resources the same material that he had found.

Betty was standing next to Randall and blushed when she said, "How marvelous, Dr. Fox, that you took the effort and time to research what was needed to aid our mission. This will help us immensely. I'll inform James and Hank immediately so they can file the necessary flight plans for our flight to EDNR."

Katie, who was silently listening to Randall's report and Betty's reply, whispered to Steve, "She's good...very good!"

Steve nodded his head in agreement. He knew that James and Hank had already filed their flight plan and Betty, who was going to accompany them in their jet, had already notified the German authorities, the Hotel Bischofshof, made their reservations, and also informed the cathedral's administrators of their arrival and official request from the queen to search for David and Marjory Seton's final resting places.

After Betty left Randall, Katie and Steve, Randall turned toward them and said, "I wonder how she knew the airport code initials for Regensburg Oberhub Airport?"

Steve replied with a straight face, "Just lucky, I guess."

Katie could hardly keep from grinning, but managed to keep a straight face. She put her arm around the University of Texas antiquities professor's waist, looked up at him and said, "We love you, Doc!"

Later in the day, Betty informed the two couples and the professor that they were going to leave Inverness Airport at 8 a.m. the next morning so they should be up by 6 a.m. and ready to leave the manor by 7 a.m.

It was going to be a short visit that would allow them to stay overnight in Regensburg and perhaps leave early enough the next day to arrive back in Scotland in time for dinner at the Manor House. Carolyn was going to arrange an early breakfast for them at six-thirty. They packed their suitcases the night before for the two-day trip.

The next morning arrived quickly and everyone who was going to Germany was in place for their early breakfast. Carolyn and Christopher's other guests were still sleeping, except for Kira. She had said goodnight to her parents, who asked her to stay in bed and sleep a little longer, but Kira got up early, left her room, crawled into bed between them, and put one arm around her father and the other around her mother and snuggled close.

When her parents woke up they were surprised to see Balthazar at the foot of their bed and Kira snuggled next to them. Balthazar, the Rood's large grey Persian cat, had been following Kira around all the day before, but now had ensconced himself where he thought he could be appreciated. He was purring softly and Kira was fast asleep.

Natalie and Dietrich woke Kira up and she rubbed the sleep from her eyes with both hands and then kissed her parents. It was then she noticed Balthazar who was slipping in between everybody. Kira hugged him and said, "He loves you both too," and then she giggled.

Natalie and Dietrich hurriedly showered and got dressed while Kira played with her new friend. Then the four of them went over to the main house for breakfast with their comrades in sleuthing. Rania laughed as her friends entered the breakfast room with Balthazar walking behind them with his tail up in the air.

"I see everyone is up!" and then everyone laughed.

Rania hugged Natalie and then they all sat down. Carolyn, who was a master chef, had already served some Quiche Lorraine to Rania, Anton, and Randall, who was busily drinking his coffee and cream. Natalie, Kira, and Dietrich sat down and Carolyn brought them all their servings of quiche with some orange juice, mixed fruit dish, and coffee. They all had cream, which was the continental fashion, except Kira who had milk with her orange juice, fruit, and quiche.

She looked up from the table and said, "Someday I'll be able to drink coffee, won't I mommy!"

After breakfast, the team of five, accompanied by Carolyn and Christopher, who had just gotten up and was still in his pajamas and robe, went down to the black Mercedes GLC class SUV that Christopher had for Betty to drive them to the Inverness Airport and their private jet. She had already put their overnight bags in the back of the SUV and after everyone said their goodbyes, the five got into the SUV and left for the airport.

Kira was waving furiously at the automobile as it descended the driveway toward the airport. She could still see her mother waving her scarf out of the window as the car disappeared into the morning haze. Kira turned to Balthazar who was standing next to her looking up as she bent down, picked him up, and whispered to him, "I hate goodbyes, don't you?"

Balthazar purred in agreement.

The jet lifted rapidly into the early morning air with Hank and James at the controls. It quickly gained its proper flight altitude as it flew towards Bavaria and Germany. The flight was uneventful and soon the aircraft was entering EDNR flight control space and started its descent toward the private airport's runway. The plane deftly landed and taxied to the private hangar arranged by the Bundesnachtrichtendienst.

As the aircraft slid into its hangar and stopped, it was met by two Bundespolizei and a tall handsome German who was part of the security team assigned to help them in their quest at the Saint Peter Dom. His name was Hans Schmidt who explained in perfect English that the curators at the Domschatz Museum had located the tombs of David Seton and his wife Marjory inside the cathedral and were waiting for them to arrive at one o'clock so they could examine their crypts.

"Well," Randall smiled at Natalie, Rania, Dietrich and Anton. "That is real German efficiency. I didn't expect it to be this easy."

Dietrich grinned and then said to Hans, "Das ist sehr gut. Vielleicht sollen wir zum hotel gehen, nicht wahr?"

Hans straightened up and agreed, "Jawohl, Herr Oberst!"

Randall was impressed and leaned over to Rania and asked, "What did he say?"

Rania replied, "Dietrich congratulated him on finding the crypts of David and Marjory Seton and then asked him if we could all go check into the hotel, freshen up, and then have lunch before we go to the cathedral. Hans then agreed and acknowledged Dietrich's rank as a colonel in the German Luftwaffe."

She and Natalie smiled as Randall took it all in and said, "Wow! The German language is really efficient to have said all that in just a few words."

Randall paused, watching Rania and Natalie laughing at him and then he said to them, "Richtig?"

They both looked at him while Dietrich smiled at Anton and they both grinned. Dietrich explained, "Randall understands German, he was just teasing both of you."

Natalie turned to her friend Rania, hunched her shoulders and said, "See what we have to put up with. Men will be boys!"

Hans loaded them all into a black Mercedes GLC class SUV and drove to the Bischofshof Hotel across the street from the cathedral, and after they checked into the hotel, he said he would meet them in the lobby at one o'clock and escort them to the cathedral to meet the curator of the Domschatz

Museum.

They all went to their respective rooms to unwind and agreed to meet for lunch at noon in the Garden Restaurant of the hotel.

After about twenty minutes, they all met in the lobby and had a wonderful lunch of German Bratwurst, salad, and a glass of beer. It was then time to cross the street and meet Hans at the entrance to the cathedral and meet the curator. His name was Johann Wolfe, and after introductions, he escorted them to the crypts of David Seton and his wife.

Their carved sarcophagi were in the floor of the cathedral opposite the bronze memorial of Prince Bishop Cardinal Philipp Wilhelm of Bavaria who was the son of William V, Duke of Bavaria and Renata of Lorraine. He was made a cardinal by Pope Clement VIII. He died in a riding accident in 1596.

The curator further explained that Philipp was a friend of David Seton and his wife and had arranged for their burials in the crypts in the floor of the cathedral. When David Seton died in 1591 after coming back from Malta, he was entombed beside his wife. His wife Marjory died in 1581 and David had gone to Malta to assuage his grief over the early death of his beloved wife.

Johann said that the strange markings over the bas relief of David Seton as a Crusader Templar Knight with his legs crossed as befits a crusader was dictated to Prince Philipp by David on his deathbed, and the prince carried out his wishes.

No one has been able to decipher what it means. Below his feet are the typical skull and crossbones of a Templar knight, but above his head is a chevron with a small circle just under the apex of the chevron and the strange phrase below it stating that "The Sword of Schönfeld will point the way." Underneath that is the phrase, "As it is above, so will it be below." A third phrase below that says "The skull is where bones are interred."

The words were engraved in English into the stone cover of the crypt with the carved effigy of David Seton, a crusading Templar knight in full battle armor and helmet with his shield and sword. His name and dates of birth and death were above the skull and crossbones, which was unusual, giving special emphasis to what was carved into the stone above his head.

Randall took several pictures of both of the crypts, the memorial plaque of Prince Philipp, and also of the general area where the crypts were located. David Seton's wife Marjory's crypt had a standard wife's cover with her name carved above the head of her effigy and the date of her birth and death and the familiar skull and crossbones beneath her feet. Her crypt indicated nobility.

They all stood in a circle looking at the effigies and wondered just what it all meant. Whatever it was, it was identical to what Dr. Browne had copied from a parchment he had found in the Vatican's Secret Archives.

Randall looked at the curator and asked, "Just what did you mean when you said that David Seton left Regensburg right after his wife died in 1581 and went to Malta and only returned to be with her in death shortly after he returned in 1591. Why did he only return to Regensburg when he knew he was dying? And why did his friend Philipp follow his request for his wife and him to be buried side-by-side in this spot opposite a bronze memorial plaque to his friend Philipp who is buried in the Munich Frauenkirche? Did Philipp request that a plaque dedicated to himself be placed opposite his dear friends after he too died?"

Dietrich asked the curator if there was anything else in the church records that might relate to this story of three friends.

Johann said, "They were all of noble birth and staunch Catholics, and obviously they kept whatever secrets they shared and took them to their graves. You know that they lived in strange times with the Reformation movements gaining strength in Europe, along with political corruption and greed coupled with family jealousies and power grabs. Nothing seemed sacred!"

Dietrich whispered to Natalie, Rania and Anton, "Only the grail!"

They all stood for what seemed a lifetime, but was only a

few minutes, and then Randall shook Johann's hand and then Han's hand and sighed, "Thank you all so much for all of your help. We're going to have to analyze what we have seen and heard. If we figure it out, we'll let you know."

Everyone shook hands and the curator walked them to the entrance of the cathedral and wished them luck and then he and Hans disappeared into the church.

They were all standing outside the cathedral on Krautermarkt straße when Rania's head suddenly lifted. She looked at Anton and then Natalie and whispered, "Don't look, but did you notice those two guys down the street about twenty meters. I just heard one of them mention us to the other. They were both speaking Arabic, but one of them sounds like he's from Saudi Arabia and the other is speaking Arabic with a Bosnian accent. Let's warn Dietrich and Randall and walk quickly to our hotel so we can tell Betty."

They walked over to Dietrich and Randall, and Rania whispered, "Don't look, but we are being watched by those two guys over there. Let's pretend we don't notice them and walk across the street to our hotel and let Betty know that we are being watched."

They turned and walked across the street to their hotel and when they entered the hotel lobby, they all breathed a sigh of relief. Randall took out his scrambled phone and punched in Betty's number.

She instantly answered the phone and said, "Yeah we know, the Bundesnachtrictendienst has had them spotted for the last hour. They arrived shortly after you entered the cathedral. One of them has just called a friend of his to let him know where you are. We have already packed all of your bags and loaded them into your SUV and I want all of you to walk through the hotel to the other side of the hotel and exit. I'll be in the SUV waiting for you to get in so we can arrest those guys. There may be some gunplay so please hurry."

Randall relayed the information that Betty had given him and they briskly walked through the hotel to the other side of the hotel and got into their black Mercedes SUV. As they pulled away from the curb there was the muffled cracks of gunfire and then police sirens.

"Just in the nick of time—just like the United States Cavalry," Betty quipped to her wards.

She deftly maneuvered the SUV through traffic, and before they knew it, they were on the highway speeding toward EDNR, Regensburg Oberhub Airport and the safety of their private jet. Suddenly, as they passed a grey Audi Q7 SUV that was parked on the side of the highway, it started and pulled in behind them. The grey Audi accelerated and quickly caught up with them.

Betty quietly remarked to her passengers that they were being followed closely by the SUV they had just passed and the driver looked like an Arab.

"Let's speed up and see if they speed up also."

Everyone turned around and could see at least three men in the Audi.

They didn't look happy.

Betty pushed the accelerator to the floor and the Mercedes responded and quickly separated from the Audi. They could see a scowl on the driver's face as he also sped up to keep pace.

One of the men in the front passenger seat of the Audi raised an AK-74 assault rifle as the front passenger side window of the Audi started to slide down.

Betty suddenly yelled, "Hold on, this is going to be a bumpy ride!"

She pushed the driver side window button and her window quickly slid down. Simultaneously, she swerved to the right and slammed on her brakes forcing the Audi to move to the left upsetting the shooter who was trying to raise his rifle into a position to fire. His window was completely down.

Betty had her .380 caliber stainless steel Walther PPK loaded with hollow point antipersonnel ammunition in her left hand and leveled at the head of her would be Arab assailant who was clearly confused by her swift maneuver. She squeezed the trigger and the Arab's bewildered face exploded in a red shower of blood.

There was confusion in the Audi as Betty's Mercedes spurted forward. She pressed her accelerator to the floor and the swerving grey Audi Q7 was left far behind. She could see the Audi SUV slowly come to a stop alongside the road. The driver had completely underestimated Betty's abilities.

Betty shouted, "It won't take them long to recover! Dietrich, alert Hank and James on your scrambled phone what has just happened and to get our jet ready to roll as soon as we arrive. We'll be at the airport in about ten minutes and they should inform the Bundespolizei to be ready for a firefight with our terrorist pursuers in a grey Audi Q7 SUV.

Betty covered the fourteen miles to the airport in record speed. Her passengers were all silent, understanding that with the maniacs that could be following them, anything could be possible. They were willing to die for Allah and did not care what innocent bystanders could be caught up in the chase.

Suddenly the airport came into sight and they could see that James and Hank had their plane on the tarmac ready to fly. The door to the craft was open when Betty pulled their SUV alongside it and they all piled out. Two Bundespolizei officers opened the back of the vehicle and grabbed their bags and rushed them into the waiting airplane.

The bags were quickly followed by their owners as the Bundespolizei helped them into the queen's private jet and closed the door. After Betty and her passengers were safely aboard, the jet's twin engines began to whine as they swiftly moved down the cleared runway and climbed rapidly into the sky, reaching for the clouds above them.

As they looked down at the airport, they could see the Bundespolizei were engaged in a pitched battle with some guys hiding behind an SUV with its tires all blown out. All of a sudden there was a terrific explosion of the gasoline tank of the burning Audi SUV. The SUV, with the terrorists beside it firing at the police, just disappeared in a blinding flash and fireball reaching into the sky.

Betty was standing, looking out the window of the jet when the blast occurred. She exclaimed, "Wow did you see that!

78

What did they want, the Holy Grail?"

She looked around at her passengers and saw that they were all white-knuckled and silent. Then they broke out in laughter realizing that she didn't know the details of their quest. They, collectively, breathed a sigh of relief.

Betty heard Dietrich say, "Yeah! That's exactly what they wanted."

He then explained to her what their quest was and that the Muslim Brotherhood was intent on destroying the relics in order to prevent a resurgence of Christianity.

Anton looked at Betty and said, "Your driving was impressive. Weren't you scared when you saw that guy raise his AK-47?"

Betty replied, "You mean AK-74 don't you. The AK-47 was phased out in 1974 and replaced with the updated AK-74 model. No, we are trained to react instinctively to all kinds of threats and receive special training in weapons, explosives, combat maneuvers, driving, and flying, among other things."

Then she smiled.

Anton whispered to Rania, "These terrorists don't know what they are up against!"

Rania nodded her head and smiled.

14 HOME AT LAST!

The queen's private jet had just landed safely at Inverness Airport and Betty and her passengers were still asleep from the rigors of the last twenty four hours. It was a soft landing and no one stirred—not even their savior, Betty. Hank poked his head around the pilot compartment door and saw that everyone was asleep and closed it, then he sat down in the copilot chair as James deftly slipped the aircraft slowly into its hangar and cut the engines.

A deafening silence penetrated the aircraft and Hank looked at James and whispered, "What do we do now? They are all still asleep?"

James lazily scratched his head and gazed at his buddy and fellow SAS officer and slowly whispered back, "Why are we whispering, the cockpit is soundproof?" And then he laughed and said "How's about we wake everybody up and go get some breakfast? We're back home and I'm hungry after flying several hours. That was really a narrow escape back there—quite a fireball. I'd love to hear how that SUV got past our net and was that close to the airstrip."

The two of them exited the cockpit and walked back to their comrade, Betty, just as she was moving around in her chair with her knees tucked close to her chest, stirred a bit more, and then opened one eye and looked at them.

"What's up? Are we back already?"

"What do you mean already? We're parked in our hangar in Inverness and the ground crew outside is probably wondering if we are all still alive."

With that, Betty quickly got up, walked swiftly to the front of the aircraft, and opened the door for the ground crew to see that all was well.

"Hi, guys," yelled Betty. "We're just a little tired after our flight and slow moving. I'll wake up our passengers, and James, Hank and I will get them and their luggage out so you can service the queen's plane. Okay?"

And then she gave the three SAS maintenance crew a thumbs up signal and disappeared back into the aircraft. By the time she arrived in the passenger cabin, Hank and James had awakened their passengers and gotten them ready for departure back to MacIntosh Manor.

Betty, who was the commander of the entire SAS team, took the initiative to suggest that they all drive to MacIntosh Manor and refresh themselves and then have breakfast with the Roods and their guests before Hank and James returned to their posts in their hotel in Inverness.

The short trip of fourteen miles from the airport in Dalcross to MacIntosh Manor passed swiftly, and when they arrived at the front entrance of the Manor, everyone including Kira Ann and Balthazar were waiting on the front steps to greet their team of five and find out how the trip went and why they were back so early.

Betty had suggested to everyone in the car not to say a word yet about their adventure in Bavaria, but to wait until after breakfast and later in the day when they could assemble in the conference room. She had a few reports to submit to Sir Richard and her military superiors before they could meet and she was sure that Natalie and Dietrich would want to talk with their daughter and check to see if Balthazar had protected her properly. She winked at the team of five and demurely smiled at the gathered crowd on the steps.

They all got out of the car and hugged, shook hands, and kissed their waiting companions.

Christopher shook Randall's hand and then whispered into his ear, "How did everything go? Did you discover what the clues meant?"

Randall whispered back, "I think so. Everything was routine so we came back early. We can talk about our trip later in the conference room."

Christopher knew his longtime friend well and he knew that Randall was in a code speak mode and that everything was not entirely well. Obviously, he had been cautioned by the SAS not to say anything until later when they were all ensconced in the conference room.

Everyone had already had their breakfast. Carolyn and Katie had laid out a nice buffet breakfast of pancakes with strawberries, honey or maple syrup, and an assortment of fruits, orange juice, coffee, cream, scones, and biscuits with butter.

The team of five with their SAS comrades sat down and leisurely ate their breakfasts as they talked casually about what they saw in the city of Regensburg, their Bratwurst lunch at the outdoor cafe at the Bischofshof Hotel, and how nice curator Johann Wolfe and Bundespolizei officer Hans Schmidt had been. Kira was on the floor playing with Balthazar who was lying on his back purring as she rubbed his chest and stroked his head and ears.

When breakfast was over, James and Hank excused themselves and said they had to be getting back to the Inverness Palace Hotel and finish their reports, take a nap, and get ready for the rest of the day. The SAS had already arrived with a car to take them back to Inverness. They bid their farewells to everyone and Debbie and Diamond Dave shook their hands and the pair of SAS agents wished them well on their trip back to Atlanta. James and Hank nodded their heads at Betty as they entered the SAS auto and then they sped away toward Inverness.

15 WHAT HAPPENED?

Betty and the three couples with Randall gathered in the conference room while Kira was outside walking in the garden with Debbie, Diamond, and Balthazar trailing behind them. Their destination was the gazebo where a nice lunch of hot dogs with potato salad, deviled eggs (Kira's favorite), potato chips, and iced tea were waiting for them. The same lunch was being served by the manor staff to everyone in the conference room where Betty was going to give her report to them and Randall was going to lead a discussion about where they were going to go from there. Betty had been invited to stay for that discussion so she could add her comments to their planning for the next steps in their quest for the grail. Sir Richard and the queen were quite interested in their adventure.

Betty began the introduction for her comments by introducing who she really was.

"Most of you have probably assumed that Sir Richard was just asking for your help in the recovery of the lost treasure from Saint Mary Chapel and that he has assigned my associates, Hank, James, and me to help you. Actually, I am the commander of a special team of MI5 assigned to aid Dr. Fox and all of you in any way possible to bring Dr. Browne's assassin to justice and recover the lost items. After consulting with Sir Richard, we feel that there is some validity in the supposition that Dr. Browne had confided to his colleague, Dr. Fox, that David Seton had left Germany after his wife died, determined to take the items to Malta.

"You see the Hospitaller Order in Bavaria was Catholic like he was and not Lutheran like the Brandenburg branch of the Order in Prussia. It was a short time after the victory of the Hospitallers over Sultan Suleiman the Magnificent and his Ottoman Turks at the Great Siege of Malta in 1565 which stopped the advance of the Muslims into Europe that David Seton's wife died.

"The English Langue had fallen into disrepair after the seizure of its property in England during the reign of King Henry VIII, and his daughter Elizabeth I continued the Protestant movement in England and wanted it for Scotland and Ireland so she could confiscate the Order's property as some of her fellow monarchs had done elsewhere in Europe.

"Scotland and Ireland had remained Catholic, and until the time of Sandilands and Knox in Scotland, the treasure had been secure in Catholic hands. When the Templar and Hospitaller properties were handed over to the newly converted Protestant, Prior Sandilands in 1560, it angered the Catholics in the Hospitaller Order that were descended from the ancient Knights Templar. They were the caretakers of the Templar lands and property in Scotland, Wales, and Ireland, as well as the remaining treasure hidden at the time of their Inquisition on Friday, October 13, 1307, in France.

"Dr. Browne and Randall believed that part of the treasure were the relics that had been in the large chest you found at Saint Mary Chapel that was empty. Dr. Browne and Randall believed the treasure was either in Bavaria or in Malta, and that's why you went to Regensburg to find out what the clues meant."

Betty opened her laptop computer, turned it on, and opened a PowerPoint presentation that she and Randall had put together.

She pushed a button on her remote control, and the five clues they had found in David Seton's letter, Dr. Browne's notes, and David Seton's effigy on his sarcophagus flashed onto the large high definition television screen that had been erected by an MI5 technical team.

They were:

1. All carved words are in English and not German.
2. Emblem of a chevron with a small circle under the apex of the chevron.
3. "The sword of Schönfeld will point the way."
4. "As it is above, so will it be below."
5. "The skull is where bones are interred."

She then continued after looking at Randall, "Randall called a colleague, Dr. James Tabor, a Ph.D. and chair of religious studies at the University of North Carolina at Charlotte. He was previously at Notre Dame and William and Mary Universities. He was a part of the investigators of the Jesus Family Tomb that was accidentally discovered during excavation for an apartment complex south of Jerusalem on the morning of Thursday, March 27, 1980. A bulldozer accidentally hit the south face of the tomb's antechamber that fell away to reveal the doorway of the tomb."

She pushed a remote button and suddenly a picture of the doorway of the tomb appeared on the screen. A sudden hush fell over the room and its assembled members.

Silence reigned for a minute and then Randall who had joined Betty beside the large screen said, "Behold the chevron with the small circle beneath its apex above the doorway to the Jesus Family Tomb! Just as it appears in the book, *The Jesus Family Tomb* by Simcha Jacobovici and Charles Pellegrino with a foreword by James Cameron."

Randall continued, "Now then, let's continue our analysis. Why are all of the words carved in English rather than German? Could it have anything to do with the English Langue that the Scottish Hospitallers with their hidden Frére Maçon Templars belonged to in Malta?"

Randall then pushed the remote button again and a picture

of the Anglo-Bavarian Langue Chapel with its bronze gate appeared on the screen.

He continued, "We know the English Langue had a chapel that had fallen into disrepair during the Reformation and the reigns of King Henry VIII and his daughter Elizabeth I. The chapel today is sealed from public entry so you can't proceed any further. It is also the entrance to the crypt of the grand masters and was once the reliquary of the langue during the time of David Seton.

"Today its altar that once sat in the oratory passage is dedicated to Saint Charles, as is the painting above it. The chapel was not restored and returned to its significance until a late eighteenth century papal bull reviving the English Langue and tying it to the Catholic Bavarian Langue with its priories of Catholic Poland and Greek Orthodox Russia during the time of Grand Master Emmanuel de Rohan-Polduc from 1775 to 1797. The chapel has borrowed from others such as the bronze gate from the icon wall of the Greek Orthodox Chapel of Our Lady of Philermos."

He continued, "What about the chevron and circle above the doorway of the Jesus Family Tomb? Could it be the sign leading to the clues? As it is above so is it below refer to the resting place of the skull or the grail or both? Or does it mean so as it is in heaven, so is it meant to be on earth? We know that skulls and bones in the first century AD were kept in ossuaries—small caskets of limestone about the size of a thigh bone in length. Several ossuaries were found in the tomb that apparently was entered sometime shortly after the First Crusade—about the time some archeologists say the Knights Templar were looking for relics in the Holy Land.

"We still are puzzled by the phrase, 'The sword of Schönfeld will point the way,' but we do know that David Seton took the ancient crusader sword of his and Dietrich's ancestor, Schönfeld, with him when he left Scotland. The carving of Schönfeld's sword and his shield with the trunk of an oak tree on it was with the carved effigy of David Seton in Regensburg."

He pushed the remote button again, and the image of David Seton's sarcophagus in Saint Peter Cathedral in Regensburg appeared.

He continued speaking, "You will note that the carving of the sword has the image of a Templar cross on the pommel of the grip of the sword. The image of an oak trunk on the shield is the coat of arms of the Schönfeld family. The priests at the cathedral have said that the sword was not buried with him, so he must have left it in Malta."

Christopher nodded his head and then broke the silence of the assembled team, "It certainly is and I'll bet that there is another clue in the Anglo-Bavarian Chapel in the Co-Cathedral of the Hospitaller Order of Saint John of Jerusalem in the city of Valetta in Malta. Carolyn and I have been there before, but only as tourists, and I don't know if I have any pictures of the chapel when Carolyn and I visited it a few years ago. We stayed at the Grand Hotel Excelsior when we were there last time."

He turned toward Carolyn and firmly said, "I'm going to be on the trip to Malta with the team this time!"

Carolyn had her arms folded, but with a smile on her face, looked back at him and replied, "I know, dear."

16 PLANNING FOR MALTA

Betty looked at Randall and exclaimed, "Well, I think we have our marching orders. Let's decide now how we are going to approach this trip to Malta. Who's going and why. What are the preparations and who do we need to notify and when? What security precautions do we need to make. Remember, the Muslim Brotherhood has Dr. Browne's notes and I'm sure they have seen what we've seen in Saint Peter Cathedral. Let's just hope they can't figure it out and we won't see them anymore. And if they do, let's hope we have a lead on them and get down to Malta and out of there before they can follow us. Okay?"

"Oh, by the way," continued Betty, "Sir Richard called and told me that a friend of his was vacationing with his wife Sally in Malta. He said his friend William Hanley was surprised and angered when he told him about the murder of their mutual friend, Dr. Browne. He said he gave him all the details that he could about the incident and that MI5 has identified his assailant as the priest Marco Baronio whose real name is Aashif al-Fayed."

"What, you're kidding me!" exclaimed Randall. "I know Bill Hanley. He and his wife, Sally Berner Hanley were introduced to me when I lectured at Purdue University in West Lafayette, Indiana, about family development in earlier civilizations in the Fall of 2011.

"They had given a gift of $3 million for the Bill and Sally Hanley Hall to nurture studies in human and family development. Hanley Hall is Purdue University's new home for discovery related to the study of families, children, adults, and gerontology related to human development in the past and the future."

"I guess that's the genesis of the name of their yacht anchored at the Royal Malta Yacht Club next to Fort Manoel Island in Marsamxett Harbor," replied Betty.

Christopher looked at Betty and said, "Why is that?"

Betty laconically replied, "The name of the yacht is *The Sally Forth*."

Everyone thought for a second and then laughed.

Betty looked around the room and then said, "I have talked with Sir Richard and we have decided that I will be in charge of the expedition to Malta. He has already contacted our Embassy in Valletta and they have made arrangements at the Malta International Airport three miles southwest of Valletta for a private hangar for our jet. An MI5 special action team is already on its way to Malta to secure and equip that hangar for our mission.

"Now then, Randall, I want you to select your team to go with us. Keep it small, only who is needed. Remember, we don't want to attract any unnecessary attention. Kate and Steve will be in charge of the command center here at MacIntosh Manor, and we need Carolyn to help them here and…"

Christopher interrupted, "I need to go with Randall and help the team."

Betty smiled and looked into Christopher's determined blue eyes and said, "As I was about to say, we need Christopher to be with the team in Malta because he is already familiar with Valletta and Malta."

Christopher sighed in relief.

She knew Christopher with his expertise in martial arts and

proven knowledge of combat would be an invaluable asset in case of danger.

She continued speaking to Randall, "Who else do we need?"

Randall was happy to have his old friend and colleague on board with the team. He remembered their pursuit of the mystery at the thirteen sycamores and the numerous times Christopher had saved the day.

"Well, we certainly need Natalie and Dietrich along with their friends Rania and Anton," he said. Then, turning to Carolyn, Katie, and Steve, he continued, "Do you mind again looking after Kira Ann while her parents are in Malta?"

Carolyn smiled, looked at her husband, and replied, "Of course not! It will be nice for Christopher to relax a bit and for us to have some peace of mind."

Christopher then looked at his guests and said to Anton and Rania, "You two have not had a chance to have a lengthy honeymoon, and it would be good for you to go to Malta with us. I want everyone to be our guests at the Grand Hotel Excelsior, where Carolyn and I have stayed. Besides, Rania is the only one who speaks six languages, including Arabic, in case we run into any of those characters."

Christopher did not know how prophetic his words were.

Betty interjected, "Thanks Christopher, but I think Sir Richard would insist that we take care of all of the expenses. After all, it's the treasure of the United Kingdom and Aashif al-Fayed that we are after!"

She continued, "We have just received some new equipment that is being offered to our agents in the field."

She held her hand up and pointed to a silver ring on her left ring finger.

"This may look like just a signet ring to the casual observer, but it is actually a miniaturized computer like an iWatch, only much smaller and with a very powerful scrambled signal. It has a high definition camera, micro-telephone system, GPS, and personal identification system that can be picked up by satellite anywhere in the world to within one-half foot of accuracy. It is voice activated and will respond only to the owner's voice and with a specific command structure that you each will program into your own specially designed ring."

Betty twisted the ring on her finger so that the signet with what appeared to be an engraved rose was facing her palm.

She then remarked, "By cupping your hand and placing it over your ear, you can clearly hear. And by cupping your hand over your mouth you can clearly speak to someone. If you cup your hand and point your palm in the direction of someone speaking, the ring with your cupped hand will act like a video phone, transmitting via satellite the conversation and the image of the person speaking back to the computer system we have set up here at MacIntosh Manor. Each of you will be issued your own ring to fit on either a middle or ring finger of your choice.

"The ladies get a rose signet ring and the men will receive a rampant lion signet ring. I'm sure the significance of the Scottish Lion and the English Rose will not be lost by anyone," she said, grinning.

"We'll measure your fingers and have the rings here tomorrow to be programmed into our computer system and then make all of the arrangements for your departure the next day. Our embassy in Valletta will be put on alert for any assistance. Mr. Hanley and his wife will be informed of your arrival and arrangements will be made for him to meet you either at your hotel or on his yacht. Okay?"

They all nodded their heads in agreement.

17 ADVENTURE IN MALTA

The team of six with Betty were settling down in their now familiar seats aboard the queen's private jet when James' head appeared from the cockpit and announced, "Please fasten your seat belts. We have been given clearance to depart for Malta and I will let you know when we have gotten to our cruising altitude of twenty thousand feet for our flight."

He smiled and then looked at Betty, winked, and said, "Hank wanted to let you know that he will take his time getting up to altitude this time."

Then he disappeared forward to join Hank.

"What was that all about?" Natalie said to Betty.

"Oh, I just mentioned to Hank and James, who were used to rapidly gaining altitude from their Navy days aboard aircraft carriers, that when they flew out of Regensburg, it was almost a vertical lift that left everyone's ears popping from the rapid change in altitude and that we didn't have to climb quite that rapidly on our way to Malta. I didn't really chastise them greatly and they understood. Actually, at the time I was really glad we escaped that fireball."

Natalie looked at her friend and remarked, "Me too!"

It was about an hour into the flight when, Rania, Natalie,

and Betty went into the galley of the aircraft to prepare the lunch that had been taken on board at Inverness.

Randall had raised his hand to volunteer to help when Rania turned around and said, "No thanks, I believe we can take care of everything." She then turned to her sister comrades and jokingly said, "These men, they think they can take care of everything."

Betty grinned, "It helps their egos if we let them think that."

The lunch they prepared was a tossed green salad with lettuce, tomatoes and avocados, sprinkled with a vinaigrette dressing, along with a pepperoni, spinach, Swiss quiche served with a light Riesling wine and chilled seltzer water. Dessert was a chocolate mousse with vanilla ice cream.

The lunch was served in the small dining area amidships. Hank had joined them, but sat with Betty off to the side since the team of five was now the team of six and the table would only comfortably seat six. Hank had not really noticed since he was hastily gobbling down the delicious repast so he could trade places with James. The conversation was light with hardly any mention of their coming adventure in Malta. Mostly, it was about Rania, her husband Anton, their recent marriage and future plans for a family, and about Anton's office where he practiced pediatrics. Anton had been an established pediatrician when he had met Rania and Natalie in Prague. This was before Natalie had gone to Marburg and met Dietrich.

Hank finished his lunch, said his goodbyes, and hurriedly vanished forward to relieve James in the cockpit so that he could have his lunch before it had grown cold. He need not have worried, for Betty had already warmed his lunch in the galley microwave, and room had been made for him at the dining table.

The last hour of their flight found Randall, Dietrich, and Anton napping in their seats while Rania, Natalie, and Betty were chatting about what they might see in Malta and what the Grand Hotel Excelsior would be like. Christopher had overheard part of their conversation as they were in a holding pattern getting ready to land at the Malta International Airport.

He assured them they would like it!

Suddenly, their plane started into a descent and within a few minutes, they were on the ground and taxiing toward their private hangar where the MI5 agents were waiting with a limousine to take them to their hotel suites selected by the United Kingdom Embassy staff for maximum security.

They were already checked into the hotel under assumed names, and they with their limousine and escort were whisked past security by the embassy staff and taken to the hotel. The security detail escorted them and their luggage to a wing of the hotel where their adjoining suites were connected to a common reception room with a fireplace, thick grey carpeting with matching overstuffed grey leather chairs, and a pair of couches. There was a full bar and a conference table with fourteen chairs surrounding it and two bouquets of multicolored cut flowers in crystal vases that were arranged in a pleasant, but not gaudy fashion. One end of the room looked out onto Marsamxett Harbour and the Royal Yacht Club on Manoel Island.

It was a beautiful day and a light breeze ruffled the white gossamer drapes hung over the open French doors. Outside on the deck was an elegant older couple looking at their yacht swaying at anchorage in the Royal Yacht Club Marina. They turned when they heard the team of six and their entourage enter the room.

The six-foot-four-inch gentleman and his wife turned to greet them. He and his wife waved and he said, "Beautiful day, isn't it? Sally and I were just looking over the harbor and talking about the Great Siege that took place here 452 years ago. It must have been something—those few knights holding off that massive horde of Ottoman Turks."

Betty advanced and shook Bill and Sally Hanley's hands and introduced everyone.

"So you are the friends of Jack who are going to track down his murderer and solve the puzzle he was working on?" Bill asked.

Randall looked at Bill and said, "We're sure going to try. I believe that Jack had it solved when he was struck down cowardly from behind."

Sally looked hopefully into Dr. Browne's friend's eyes and said, "We are prepared to do whatever needs to be done to make sure the cowardly assassin receives his just deserts. We don't want him and his followers to believe that justice will not be done!"

Betty replied, "You and the queen are on the same page. This is going to be a maximum effort and we appreciate your feeling and concern. I have been told, Mr. Hanley, that you want to join our team. Is that so?"

"Yes, ma'am, I do. I want to see that S.O.B. go to his seventh heaven!"

"Well sir, I can't promise you that, but we'll certainly keep you informed of our progress, and if we get our hands on him, you can be assured that you will be able to meet him."

Bill glared with revenge, and Betty could see the grief in his eyes over the loss of his friend.

"Don't worry sir, Aashif al-Fayed's days are numbered."

Sally patted her husband's arm and everyone gathered around Sally and Bill to express their condolences.

Presently, the lunch that Sally and Bill had ordered for everyone from the Admirals Landing Brasserie at the hotel arrived. It was a repast of Scottish scallops and cauliflower with duck and foie gras. It was accompanied by cacciucco soup served with pasta and risotto that included garganelli and acquarello risotto of prawn and portobello mushroom with cherry tomatoes and aged grana padano shavings, and chicken and carrots. For dessert, Sally had selected opera torte of layered dacqouise, praline butter cream and sao thome ganache kalamansi curd, coffee ice cream, and citrus salad or raspberry and mascarpone mousse apple tart, vanilla sauce, and 'fior di latte' ice cream. Various wines and whiskeys along with beer and sparkling water were available to choose.

When everyone was finished with their meal and the table was cleared by the hotel staff, Betty announced that they would all be free that evening to roam the hotel. She admonished them not stray too far since they were scheduled to go to the Saint John's Co-Cathedral the next morning after they finished their breakfasts that were to be served in their individual suites. She suggested they assemble in the reception room for the trip around 10 a.m.

Sally and Bill said they would like to see them tomorrow evening for dinner and perhaps they could all come to their yacht at the Royal Yacht Club. That sounded acceptable to everyone and they agreed to meet there around 8 p.m. Sally and Bill said their farewells and departed to the Grand Hotel Excelsior Marina where their speedboat was docked.

The weary adventurers spent the evening strolling through the various shops and arcades, indoor and outdoor swimming pools, and finally landed at the outside Tiki Bar and Restaurant alongside a large outdoor pool on the shore of Marsamxett Harbour overlooking the Royal Yacht Club and the myriad of sparkling lights of Manoel Island.

The Tiki Restaurant offered a variety of salads and they decided to all get the bruschetta platter followed by each one having a different pasta so they could get a taste of all of the different ones. They chose the tagliatelle vongole, the raviolacci sea bass, the strigoli "surf and turf," the bigoli lamb, the gnocchi porcini, and the risotta butternut squash. They each chose an appropriate wine and then proceeded to exchange portions of what they each had ordered. After they finished their meals, they decided on cappuccino for everyone and a quiet look at the sailboats leisurely returning from a day on the Mediterranean.

They then returned to their suites for a good night's sleep before resuming their adventure the next day.

Rania and Anton slowly opened the door to their suite. Anton, who was six-feet-two-inches tall with dark wavy hair, sparkling blue eyes with an impish glint, a perfect smile and an athletic build, leaned down and scooped up his beautiful wife, who resembled the actress Audrey Hepburn, and pushed through the door with his wife giggling.

He pushed the door shut with one foot as Rania whispered,

"What are you doing?"

Anton sheepishly answered, "I'm merely taking Dr. Rood's advice and pretending it's our honeymoon."

She looked up at him and sighed, "Why pretend?"

And with that Anton carried her over to their bed where the covers had already been drawn down and the inevitable piece of gold wrapped chocolate left on both pillows. He laid her tenderly on the bed, kissed her passionately on her lips, and slowly started to undress her. She responded by unbuttoning his shirt. Soon they were naked and caressing each other as they slowly made love.

It seemed like hours, but the clock said they had only taken thirty minutes in their lovemaking when Rania reached over and turned out the bedside light. It was then they noticed the light of the full moon shining through the French doors of their room. They rose from the bed and walked over to the light that bathed their naked bodies and exposed the outside deck that was shielded from the other rooms by a stuccoed partition on either side.

On the deck was a padded chaise lounge chair with a glass topped side table with an umbrella and two adjoining chairs. There was a soft blanket on the chaise lounge as if someone had anticipated their lovemaking. Rania looked up into her husband's eyes as the soft evening breeze caressed them and they began their lovemaking again until they finally laid down entwined in each other's arms and gently fell asleep.

The first ray of the morning sun peeked over the deck's bannister and caught Anton's eyes. He blinked and then slowly opened his eyes realizing they had spent the entire night wrapped in each other's arms. He looked down at Rania's gentle face and kissed her on her eyes. As she blinked, he kissed her on her mouth and then whispered, "Good morning, I love you."

She blinked again, getting her bearings, kissed her husband and hugged him. Then she whispered, "I love you too." They held each other for a couple minutes more, not wanting the magic of their embrace to stop.

They slowly got up, wrapped the blanket around themselves and looked at the clock. It declared that it was 7 a.m. and they could go to bed. They looked at each other and smiled, then eagerly jumped back into their bed.

18 THE ANGLO BAVARIAN LANGUE CHAPEL

Everyone had gathered in the reception room ready to go to the Saint John Co-Cathedral and search the Anglo Bavarian Langue Chapel for the clues that might reveal the whereabouts of the missing artifacts from Saint Mary Chapel at the thirteen sycamores on Mount Lothian. The British Embassy had made arrangements with the Maltese government and the curators of the co-cathedral to open the bronze gates of the chapel and allow the three MI5 agents and the six members of the research team to inspect the chapel and see if they could find the clues mentioned on David Seton's sarcophagus.

Betty took immediate charge of the group and they went downstairs to the British Embassy's Jaguar F-Pace 35t AWD SUV that was waiting patiently in front of their hotel. It was large enough to carry the team of six, but Betty, Hank and James had to follow behind in a British Embassy XF sedan. They drove down the Triq L- Lassedju L K-Bir to the Triton Fountain through the city gates down Triq IR Repubblika to Triq San Qwann and turned right. In front of them and to the left was the front of the co-cathedral and a smiling curator ready to escort them to the Anglo Bavarian Chapel. The cathedral was a stunning example of sixteenth century High Baroque architecture. It was commissioned four years after the death of Fra' Jean Parisot de Vallette, the grand master of the Order of Saint John, Knights Hospitaller. It was he who was commander of the knights and Maltese citizens who defended Malta successfully in the Great Siege of 1565 and saved Europe from invasion by the Ottoman Turks and Sultan Suleiman the Magnificent.

Fra' Jean Parisot de Vallette laid the cornerstone of the city that would be named after him. The enormous structure façade is made of limestone and has a fortress like appearance. On each corner of the entrance façade are small fountains topped respectively with a lion and a unicorn. The large entrance doors are guarded by two massive pillars supporting a balcony opening onto the third floor.

They all stepped through the front entrance into the highly decorated nave from which the chapels of the various langues extend out on both sides of the very wide nave. Every inch of the nave's floor space is taken up with intricately designed flat inlaid marble tombstones of the knights of the Order.

As you walk down the nave on the left is firstly the Chapel of Italy, then France, and then at the end of the row is the Chapel of the Anglo Bavarian Langue, once the reliquary of the English Langue after the English and Scottish Reformation occurred in the sixteenth century. It wasn't until the Bavarian Langue with its Polish Priory and Russian Priory in Saint Petersburg were attached to the English Langue when it was revived in the late eighteenth century by a papal bull that was issued that the chapel regained its significance and glory.

The chapel is sealed from public entry by locked bronze gates originally from the icon wall of the Greek Orthodox Chapel of Our Lady of Philermos. The chapel acts also as the entrance to the crypt of the grand masters. The altar of the chapel once sat in the Oratory Passage and is dedicated to Saint Charles, as is the painting above it. Off to the right of the altar is an alcove with a statue of a crusading Hospitaller knight in thirteenth century armor and helmet with a red shield emblazoned with the white Maltese cross of the Order on his left shoulder and images of an oak trunk on his gauntlets, and holding a crusader sword with a blood red wooden grip wrapped with a silver cord and a circular pommel displaying an inlaid Maltese cross in his hands. The knight is wearing a red mantle with a white cross, and his hands are folded as if in prayer and pointing to the relic cabinet just below the painting of Saint Charles being presented to the Virgin Mary and the Christ Child. The praying hands holding the sword appeared to be pointing under the painting to the brass handles on the cabinet doors with an emblem of a chevron with a circle under the apex.

The group, with the curator leading the way, quietly walked behind him as he explained each of the chapels and their story. Finally, they reached the padlocked gate of the Anglo Bavarian Langue and the curator carefully unlocked the padlock and let the chain holding the closed gate fall to the marble floor with a loud crash.

He turned to his audience and exclaimed, "I'm sorry for that noise. This gate has not been opened for years."

Betty assured him it was okay and that all they wanted to do was go inside and just take a look.

The curator smiled and then said, "It's alright to look, but don't touch anything."

Everyone nodded their head and they walked inside and started to examine everything. Christopher was cocking his head to one side as he looked at the statue of the knight in armor. He then turned and spied Dietrich and Randall over at the left corner of the chapel.

He slowly walked over to them and whispered to them, "Do you guys notice anything strange about that knight?"

Randall replied, "Well, let's see, he's wearing the armor and helmet of a knight from the Crusades. He is a Hospitaller. The sword is a crusader sword as is the shield. No, it looks authentic."

"What about you, Dietrich?"

"Well, everything looks okay…wait a minute, look at the oak trunk emblems on his gauntlets."

"Lower your voice," cautioned Christopher.

"Isn't that an image of an oak trunk at a 45-degree angle?"

Randall and Dietrich's eyes widened and they both whispered, "It's the coat of arms of the Schönfeld family"

Christopher whispered to them, "That is Schönfeld's sword that David Seton took from the Saint Mary Chapel. That raised brass emblem that the knight's praying hands and sword are pointing to is a key to open the cabinet probably containing a first century Jerusalem ossuary, and I'll bet the skull and the grail are inside it!"

Randall bent down and whispered, "Bingo! We found it! If that key is pressed into the cabinet, I'll bet the doors will open and reveal the ossuary we are looking for. Calm down, I'll go over and quietly explain to Betty that we have discovered what we came here for. Okay?"

They both nodded their approval and Randall sauntered over to Betty and touched her elbow to get her attention and then whispered, "We've found what we came here for."

Betty's head quickly jerked around and she stared into Randall's bluish hazel eyes. She could see that he was telling her the facts.

"Okay," she whispered. "Let's be nonchalant and not tip off anyone yet. Let's casually thank the priest for his assistance and go back to the hotel and plan our next move. I need to talk with Sir Richard about this before we do anything else."

"Okay, I'll tell Christopher and Dietrich," whispered Randall.

Betty went over to the curator and explained to him that they had seen enough and that her majesty, the queen, and Sir Richard deeply appreciate his help. She gathered her flock together and Natalie, Rania, and Anton were surprised they were going to return to the hotel so soon and not look around the cathedral some more.

They left the co-cathedral, shook the curator's hand,

thanked him for his courtesy, and climbed into their cars.

They did not notice the priest standing to the far right side of the entrance to the co-cathedral carefully examining the artwork carving of the stone unicorn fountain. The priest was Marco Baronio who was none other than Aashif al-Fayed who had murdered Dr. Browne!

19 THE KIDNAPPING

As the team drove back to the Grand Hotel Excelsior, Betty was telling Hank and James that they had found what they were looking for and she had to get permission from Sir Richard to go back to the co-cathedral at night, break into the cathedral, open the gate to the Anglo Bavarian Chapel, remove Schönfeld's sword, replace it with another, remove the contents from the ossuary cabinet and replace it with another ossuary, and lock the gate so it would appear that nothing was taken. She remarked that the padlock on the gate was so simple that she could unlock it with one of her hairpins!

All that could be done easily and what she needed was only a twenty-minute pause in the cathedral's security system. Could MI5 make that happen without arousing anyone's attention? That was the question she needed to have answered.

Meanwhile in the Jaguar F Pace SUV, Christopher, Dietrich, and Randall were explaining their discovery that matched the riddle that Dr. Browne had found in the Vatican's Secret Archives. Everyone was elated, but they had to choose just a few to go back tonight. But who?

When they all assembled in the reception room, Betty took

charge and said, "I guess everyone knows by now that we have probably found the Holy Grail, Schönfeld's sword, the skull, and its ossuary. Technically, all of these things are the property of the United Kingdom that were illegally taken from Scotland in 1572, and we are going to merely return them to their rightful owner. We are therefore doing a service for mankind."

Randall interrupted, "But David Seton was a knight of Scotland, an independent country at the time, who was taking the relics, albeit stolen by the Templars from Constantinople, the capital of the now no longer existing Byzantine Empire, by the now no longer existing Knights Templar that sought refuge within the Scottish branch of the Knights Hospitaller as the Frérè Maçon whose branches still exist and whose home was within the English Langue and whose members and chapel existed at the time David Seton took them to Malta. Since the Knights Templar had joined with the Knights Templar at that time, he was merely returning the relics to their rightful owner at that time!"

"Whew!" Betty exclaimed. "Slow down. Today, they still belong to the UK and we are taking them back."

By this time, everyone was totally confused and Christopher made the argument even more confused by saying, "Don't forget that Barbara Frale discovered the Chinon Parchment in the Vatican Secret Archives which said that Pope Clement V had absolved the Templars of all charges of heresy and therefore the Knights Templar were illegally deprived of their existence and property that still existed at the time of David Seton and through the Frérè Maçon knights within the Hospitaller Order of Saint John in Scotland and therefore still existed as a hidden branch of the Knights Templar as proclaimed by the Saint Clair and the Seton families and Mary, Queen of Scots and her mother, Mary of Guise!"

By this time, everyone's head was spinning until Betty clarified everything by simply explaining, "Our Queen Elizabeth II is the sovereign head of our reconstituted Order of Saint John which inherited the Chapel of the Anglo Bavarian Langue and its properties and the island of Malta through the

Treaty of Paris. She later granted the freedom of Malta under the Malta Independence Act passed by the British Parliament in 1964 with the queen as its sovereign head and then to the Republic of Malta which is now an independent republic nation within the British Commonwealth of Nations. Simply stated, possession is nine-tenths of the law and we and our queen intend to possess what is now residing inside the chapel!"

Betty smiled and then simply turned to the issue of how they were going to break into the chapel that night and deliver the goods to the queen.

"I believe that the team going to the chapel tonight should be Christopher, Randall, Hank, James, and me, as well as Rania. The Maltese language is a mixture of Italian and Arabic from the time of the conquest of the islands by the Muslim Berbers in 870 AD until the conquest of the islands by the Normans in 1091. Since Rania speaks several languages including Arabic and Italian and can understand the complex Maltese language, she should be part of our team in case we run into any Maltese policemen. Okay?"

Anton dropped his head, but agreed when Betty assured him that everything would be okay. Sir Richard had arranged for the security system at the co-cathedral to be shut down, without the authorities in Valletta realizing it, for a half hour starting at 8 p.m.

Everyone else would accept Sally and Bill Hanley's invitation to dine tonight on their yacht at the Royal Yacht Club. They should all plan to be dressed for dinner and meet back in the reception room and then gather in front for the British Embassy SUVs to take them by ferry to Fort Manoel and the Royal Malta Yacht Club Marina. Bill would be there at the club to escort them from the clubhouse to his yacht.

Meanwhile, the MI5 team with Rania, Randall, and Christopher would arrange to be at the entrance to the co-cathedral at precisely 8 p.m.

They then retired to their rooms to rest and contemplate the evening. Anton was still concerned. He was overly protective of his wife because of everything she had been through from her troubled childhood to their hidden marriage and escape from the Muslim Brotherhood and her brother and father. Rania was cheerful and explained that he shouldn't worry because she was made of stern stuff and could endure any hardship as long as they were together.

The time finally arrived and they all gathered in the reception room. Everyone in the yacht party looked their best in formal dinner attire, and the cathedral team looked very casual in their break-in attire.

Betty spoke, "Okay, we all have our duties understood. Right? Everyone have their rings on and understand how to communicate with each other and with Kate, Steve, and Carolyn back at MacIntosh Manor?'

Everyone nodded their heads in the affirmative. They had each taken the time that afternoon to practice communication with their smart rings and were ready for the evening's activities.

The dinner team left first, going down to the lobby and the entrance of the Grand Hotel Excelsior where they were met by the British Embassy drivers with their SUVs. As soon as everyone was comfortably seated, the SUVs departed for the ferry and their short trip to the Royal Malta Yacht Club.

Betty and her MI5 team with Christopher and Randall left the reception room individually, with Betty and Hank carrying one of the duplicate items collected by British Embassy staff that afternoon from various shops in Valletta. Betty carried the duplicate sword in its inconspicuous box; Hank carried a white soft stone duplicate ossuary approximately 70 centimeters long and 35 centimeters high and wide that the Embassy had found in a shop dealing with fake ancient artifacts. They all regrouped in the parking lot where the Embassy Jaguar XF sedan was parked. James opened the passenger side doors on the left side of the sedan and climbed into the driver's side on the right. They quietly drove to the co-cathedral, parked in front of the entrance, and waited until a couple of minutes past eight. Then Betty, Christopher, Randall, and Hank got out of the sedan and casually walked up to the entrance of the cathedral after checking that no one was watching.

Christopher, Randall, and Hank huddled in a semicircle around Betty as she quickly picked the lock and opened the door—no alarm went off. Great! They were all instantly in and closed the door behind them, turned on their flashlights, and walked down the nave they had seen that morning until they were opposite the Anglo Bavarian Langue Chapel with its locked bronze gate. Betty quickly picked the lock and they were in!

Meanwhile, outside the cathedral a 2017 black Audi A4 four-door sedan pulled up behind the car James and Rania were sitting in and two priests got out and walked over to the car—one priest on Rania's side and the other on James' side.

Rania looked at James and said, "Don't worry, I'll take care of this."

Then she pushed the window button and lowered her window to speak to the priest.

The priest asked in Italian, "What are you doing here?"

Rania replied in Italian, "We're just admiring the artisanship of the façade. It's so beautiful!"

James was just reaching under his shirt to grip his M9A3 17-shot Beretta handgun when the other priest pulled a .380 caliber PPKS with a sparrow silencer from under his coat and pointed it at Rania.

"I don't think so," he said in perfect English. "Now if the two of you will get out of your automobile and get into our car we can resolve this issue. Don't make the mistake of trying to escape. Come peacefully and no one will be hurt."

James looked at Rania and said, "Do as he says," as he activated the GPS of his ring.

Rania and James got out of their car and the second priest wrapped duct tape around their arms just above their wrists. He removed James' M9A3 Beretta from his waist holster, and he motioned for them to get in the back seat of their sedan. The second priest got in the passenger front seat and turned around facing them while he pointed his gun at Rania.

"We are going for a little ride, so just relax and everything will be fine," he said.

Looking back at Raina and James the first priest said, "That's right, I am Father Marco Baronio and the church has some questions we need to have answered."

Then he turned to the second priest and said in Arabic, "They should fetch a nice price in the slave market in Tunis, don't you think?"

A horrified look appeared in Rania's eyes as she thought of her own mother's kidnapping as a college student so long ago. Tears started to form in her eyes and she fought them back bravely and stared at James.

He could sense that something bad was happening, but kept quiet. He had activated the alert signal and knew that MI5 was now tracking them by satellite.

20 THE RECKONING

Betty had just entered the Anglo Bavarian Chapel when she realized that the alert signal had been sent and they were all now being tracked by the British MI5 satellite tracking system and they only had another fifteen minutes to get out of the co-cathedral.

"Let's get a move on and get out of here, something has happened and we don't have much time. Grab the sword and ossuary and replace them. We can examine them later."

Christopher, Randall, and Hank agreed as they deftly accomplished their assignments.

Christopher pushed the key, grasped the brass handles on the two doors of the ossuary cabinet, and looked inside. His flashlight revealed a white stone ossuary. He took it out of its resting place and breathed, "It's heavy. There is more than just a skull and a cup inside."

He swiftly laid the ossuary onto the floor and put the empty replacement ossuary into the cabinet and closed the doors. A clicking sound was heard as the doors closed.

Christopher picked up the ossuary on the floor and whispered to everyone, "I've got it. Let's get out of here!"

Dietrich had already retrieved his ancestor's sword and

replaced it with the duplicate sword. Betty locked the bronze gate of the chapel and they rapidly ran to the entrance door of the co-cathedral and exited it. Betty locked the door and turned around to go to their sedan.

Hank had already reached their sedan and looked horrified into the empty car and said, "Look! James and Rania aren't in the car—what's going on?"

They all looked at each other and ran to the empty embassy sedan. Hank opened the trunk of the car and they placed Schönfeld's sword under a blanket in the trunk and placed the ossuary into the box the duplicate had been in. They carefully wrapped all of the objects in some blankets they had in the trunk to secure the confiscated items. They then got into the sedan and Betty called Steve in Scotland on her scrambled cell phone.

"What's going on, Steve?"

Steve replied, "James activated the alarm system and we now have a visual and an audio on what's going down. Rania and James have been kidnapped and we are tracking them by satellite. They are now on a ferry crossing Marsans Harbour towards Manoel Island and Fort Manoel and the Royal Malta Yacht Club Marina."

Betty replied, "You're kidding, that can't be right."

"Yes, we are certain, the visual and audio we are receiving has been processed and confirm they have been captured by two fake priests, one of whom is Aashif al Fayed posing as Father Marco Baronio—the same guy who murdered Professor Browne."

"Where are they going? Does the Muslim Brotherhood have a ship anchored at the Royal Yacht Club Marina?"

Steve replied, "We're checking now. It appears they do, but we don't know which slip."

Betty could hear Katie in the background saying to Steve, "They've stopped. They are definitely at the marina and we are zeroing in with the satellite cameras. Yes, we can now see them. There are four people, three men and a woman. It looks like two of the men are dressed as priests and the other man and woman are handcuffed—no they are bound by duct tape at the wrists.

"They are now on board a yacht and being ushered below deck. Wait a minute and we'll have the name of the yacht and the slip number. We can see that there is an empty slip next to the yacht."

There was a pause, and Betty looked at Hank as he started the sedan and headed for the ferry that would take them to the yacht club. If they hurried, they could just make the ferry's next trip to Manoel Island.

Betty calmly said to Hank, "Don't break any speed limits. We don't have time to explain to the local police or magistrates what is going on."

Hank slowed down and replied, "Yeah, I know. It's just that we promised Anton that no harm would come to Rania."

"I know you're anxious, we all are," she calmly said, "If we have to, we can be there in the nick of time."

Suddenly, Katie's voice came back on line, "The yacht's name is *The Four Winds* and the slip number is 41."

Betty replied, "We're almost to the ferry landing and we are in time to get on board for the next sailing. Hank is just now driving onto the ferry."

Steve said, "Yes, we can see you now. We'll be back with you when you get to the yacht club. I presume you're going to Bill Hanley's yacht, *The Sally Forth*, aren't you? It's in slip 3. We'll start the motion to allow you to have the Hanleys move their yacht alongside *The Four Winds* and you can take it from there. Okay?"

"Will do," replied Betty. "I'll be back with you and our plan of action as soon as we arrive at *The Sally Forth*."

Meanwhile, below decks of *The Four Winds*, Aashif al-Fayed was interrogating his two captives.

"Why were the two of you sitting in front of the cathedral? You and your friends were there this morning. Were they coming back from somewhere to meet you?"

Rania replied in English, "My husband was supposed to meet us there after he went shopping with his friend Hank for a picture of the cathedral he had seen in a nearby shop. They are probably worried that we weren't in our car and that we might have gotten out to search for them and are now lost. They no doubt have notified the police and they are looking for us."

Aashif turned to his fellow captor, grinned and said in Arabic, "Well, they are going to be searching a long time—a lifetime." And then they both laughed.

Aashif turned to James and then to Rania and demanded, "Stand up and turn around slowly, I want to take a good look at both of you."

James and Rania slowly stood up, looked at each other and then turned slowly around and started to sit down.

Aashif grabbed Rania's arm and held her upright. "Not you, stand up tall. How tall are you? About five feet seven?"

Rania replied, "Yes, that's correct. You sound like someone trying to judge someone auditioning for a part in a play."

Aashif smiled, then demanded, "Raise your arms above your head and turn around again, slowly. I want to see your figure again."

Rania complied and Aashif told her to sit down, and then he turned to his friend and said in Arabic, "I may want to keep her myself. She is beautiful!"

Rania pretended not to understand, but she had a desperate look in her eyes as she turned toward James. He could see the desperation in her face and wondered what was going on and why did their captors seem to be waiting for someone else to arrive.

The ferry docked and Hank drove their sedan onto the dock and rapidly drove down the road to the yacht club. They entered the club's parking lot, parked their car, and went into the club. The British Embassy security team was there to greet them and ask them to follow them to slip three. They carried Heckler and Koch MP-5 9mm submachine guns and looked like they knew how to use them. They had grim looks on their faces as Betty greeted them and flashed her credentials for them to see.

The three men softened their look and snapped to attention as they recognized that Betty was a superior officer and automatically in charge of the operation. They had been informed they would be met by a colonel in the MI5 section of British International Security.

Betty explained they were going to talk with Mr. Hanley, an American industrialist, a friend of Professor Browne and a knight of the American Priory of the Queen's Order of Saint John. They understood and escorted Betty and her team to Bill's yacht where he, his wife, and their dinner guests were about to be served dessert.

They looked remarkably out of place with everyone else in formal dinner attire, but Betty carefully laid out what had happened and what was about to happen.

She explained that MI5 was monitoring everything and she needed Bill to have his crew weigh anchor and sail their yacht to slip 40 with his guests continuing their dinner. When they enter slip 40 and his crew moors his boat, he will pretend to be drunk and walk over to the neighboring slip 41 and *The Four Winds* and engage the crew in idle conversation, distracting them so the British Embassy Security Force can move into position to arrest and secure the crew. They will then quietly take positions on *The Four Winds* to allow her and Christopher to go below decks and arrest Aashif al-Fayed and his friend.

Bill looked at her and said, "Is that the S.O.B. that killed Jack?"

Betty replied, "Yes, it is, but we can handle it."

Bill looked determinedly into her eyes and said, "It's my ship, I'm the captain and I'm going with you!"

Betty could see that Bill was deadly serious and there was no stopping him. She agreed and said, "All right, but stick close to me."

"Closer than flypaper," he replied.

Betty thought for a second at Bill's reply and then she smiled and thought to herself, "That's what cowboys in Omaha, Nebraska, say when they are determined."

Bill disappeared into his stateroom and then reappeared

with a Colt M1911 A1 .45 ACP caliber pistol.

Betty remarked, "Do you know how to use that?"

"Damn betcha!" Bill said.

Betty thought to herself, "He'll be a good backup."

Bill's crew deftly maneuvered his yacht into slip 40 and secured the mooring lines when Christopher and Bill appeared on deck with Bill's arm around Betty who by this time was dressed in one of Sally's evening gowns and Christopher in a tuxedo. The three of them seemed to be drunk with Betty and Bill appearing to be affectionate with each other as they waved to the two crewmen on the deck of *The Four Winds*.

Christopher had his Dawson Precision Practical Advantage .40 caliber pistol in his belt holster beneath his coat. Bill had his .45 caliber ACP Colt pistol secured in his belt, hidden by his coat and Betty had her .380 caliber stainless steel Walther PPK in her small purse in her left hand. Bill had his arm around Betty's waist as they walked onto the platform connecting the wharf with the deck of *The Four Winds*. The two crewmen moved toward Bill who waved at them and then tried to drunkenly put his left arm around one of the crew members. The crewmen smiled at them and before they could react, Bill had his Colt pistol in his right hand and pointed at the crewman's head. At the same instant Betty had removed her pistol from her bag and was holding it against the forehead of the other crewmen. Christopher had drawn his pistol and was leading the trio to the door leading to the yacht's salon.

The British Embassy security team appeared and took the two men into custody and asked them if there were any more crew members on board. They said there weren't—the other crew members were in town for the night—and they were expecting, sometime tomorrow, an important person from Benghazi to arrive.

Christopher motioned for Betty and Bill to follow him and they quietly went below decks where they heard Rania scream as Aashif was trying to make advances toward her. Christopher burst through the door to the cabin, delivered a blow with his left fist to the head of the second priest and knocked him unconscious, with Betty close behind. Christopher pointed his Dawson at the fallen priest. She had her PPK leveled at Aashif, who had grabbed Rania with his arm around her neck and his pistol in his right hand was now pointed at Rania's head. A red dot from the laser sight of Betty's PPK illuminated Aashif's left ear. Bill was standing in the doorway, filling it with his tall frame. He was standing in front of Aashif, blocking any exit. He had drawn his Colt .45 pistol and had it aimed at Aashif's head.

Aashif's eyes were wild and he was confused. He screamed at Christopher, Bill, and Betty to lay down their guns or he was going to shoot Rania.

Betty calmly said, "If you do, you son of a bitch, I'll shoot you where it hurts the worst and you'll be able to sing as a soprano!"

Bill was aiming his .45 Colt at Aashif's nose when Aashif said, "You think I'm a coward, I'll show you!" as he took his pistol from Rania's head and started to turn it toward James who was tied up in a chair to his right and completely helpless. Aashif was starting to pull the trigger as Rania bent her knees and pushed her arms upward underneath his arm, uncovering him. The sudden move caused Aashif's shot to go wildly past James. Simultaneously, Bill squeezed the trigger of his Colt that was now pointed at Aashif's left ear as Betty pulled the trigger of her PPK that was now aimed at the back of Aashif's head. The two shots hit Aashif's at the same time and his head exploded into a shower of blood and brains that covered the wall behind him and threw his body back against the wall and away from Rania, sparing her the shower of blood.

Betty looked at Bill and said, "Does that even the score for his killing your best friend?"

Bill looked at her with a sudden calm that had come over him and he replied, "Almost."

21 WHERE TO NOW?

Rania was lying on the deck of the cabin, crying as Betty slid down on the deck with her, put her arms around her quaking shoulders, and held her close, whispering to her, "Your husband Anton is here."

Anton had entered the cabin just as Betty had put her arms around his wife. Rania looked up and saw her husband smiling as he bent down and picked her up into his arms. He whispered tenderly into her ear, "I love you my darling, more than my life itself. I'm so happy we found you and you're okay."

Rania looked up into his eyes filled with tears and whispered back, "I'll never let you go. I love you so much."

Bill looked over to the reunited couple and thought to himself, "I know exactly how they feel. I feel the same toward Sally."

The embassy security team took charge of the situation, and Bill, Betty, James, Rania, and Anton gathered themselves together and walked over to *The Sally Forth* where they were greeted by their friends. They all embraced each other and remarked how glad they were at their narrow escape.

Bill put his arms around his wife Sally and held her tightly. He then looked down and kissed her unabashedly and said, "I had not realized how much you mean to me and how much I love you until a few minutes ago when I thought I might never see you again."

Sally looked up at her husband, squeezed his hand and put her arms around his neck pulling him down and kissed him. She then whispered, "Me too."

The friends had all said their goodbyes and returned to the Grand Hotel Excelsior, the local police and the Malta National Security Forces had impounded *The Four Winds* and taken into custody Aashif's friend and collected Aashif's remains, and Sally and Bill had sailed their yacht back to slip 3 when word came from Sir Richard that the queen was delighted that her friend Dr. Browne's assassin had been dealt with, but she was curious about the treasure. Betty and Steve assured Sir Richard that a full report would be forthcoming.

Natalie and Anton had their arms around Rania as everyone trudged into their reception room in the Grand Hotel Excelsior. Rania had pretty well collected herself after her ordeal and Hank and Christopher had brought the ossuary and Schönfeld's sword up from their sedan and deposited them on the table. Everyone sat down and stared at the objects as they reviewed in their minds what they had all gone through to come to this point of reckoning. They were about to open the ossuary and view the skull of John the Baptist and the Holy Grail of Jesus Christ!

After staring at the relics, Randall stood up and said, "If we are going to be able to all at least get a good night's sleep, I better open the ossuary and see what's inside. It certainly feels heavy."

As Randall lifted the lid of the ossuary and looked inside and everyone leaned forward to see, they all simultaneously gasped, "It's a partial skeleton!"

Randall noted the skeleton with the femurs crossed, but no skull, and the right arm was missing. No grail. He saw a couple of teeth which meant that a skull had probably resided within the ossuary at one time, but was no longer there. Where was the grail? David Seton's letter was explicit. What could have happened between 1591 and the present to account for the discrepancy? Whose skeleton is it? Is it that of a man or a woman? What is the age of the skeleton? The ossuary certainly looks like First Century AD. There is writing on the side of it, but what does it say? The chevron and the circle certainly match the description of the ossuaries described in the book, *The Jesus Family Tomb*. What do we need to do next? Should we call in Professor James D. Tabor, chair of the Department of Religious Studies at the University of North Carolina at Charlotte?

These were all questions they couldn't answer tonight.

Randall said, "This is not a disappointment, merely another riddle to unravel. Let's all go to bed and thank our lucky stars that Rania and James are safe and that we are all still alive."

The team looked at each other and realized the wisdom in what Randall had just said and they all agreed it was time to call it a very long day. They then waved at each other and went to their suites after agreeing to meet the next morning about 10 a.m. after breakfast in their suites and before getting everything together for their 1 p.m. flight back to Inverness with their discoveries and return to Scotland with at least a part of their treasure. But where do they go from here?

Anton picked up his still fragile wife after her ordeal and carried her into their suite. He laid her down on their bed, noting a few blood stains on her clothes, and said, "Let's get rid of these clothes along with the memory of your ordeal and wash the last few hours away by taking a shower together?"

Rania looked anxiously into her husband's blue eyes and said, "Let's do."

They both took their clothes off and Rania threw hers to the side and said, "I never want to see those again or ever think of that awful Aashif al-Fayed ever again. I want to erase his face and words from my memory forever!"

22 THE ANSWERS

The queen's jet with its passengers had just touched down at Inverness Airport and entered into its private hangar. Everyone was happy to be back home and were ready to get back to MacIntosh Manor and their friends. Betty, Hank, and James had to turn in their reports and await new orders from Sir Richard and MI5, and Natalie and Dietrich were anxious to see Kira Ann. Rania and Anton just wanted to spend time in Carolyn's garden and enjoy the relaxation, while Christopher could hardly wait to be with Carolyn.

As for Randall, he wanted to talk to Dr. Tabor about the events in Malta and take a better look at Schönfeld's sword and the bones and teeth in the ossuary, as well as the ossuary itself.

He knew that between David Seton's death in 1591 and the present day, the most momentous upheaval for the Order of Saint John was in 1798 when Napoleon arrived at Malta and forced the Order off the island and into a diaspora that exists to this very day.

The individual langues of the previous independent and Sovereign Hospitaller Order of Saint John are spread all over the world with some of them being absorbed by various monarchies into royal orders such as the Spanish and the

Portuguese langues.

Some, like the remnants of the Scottish and Irish branches of the English Langue, found refuge in the German Langue, and then later into the Anglo Bavarian Russian Langue connected with Czar Paul I, the Romanov family, and after World War II, with King Peter II of Yugoslavia.

The Italian Langue which was protected by the pope eventually took refuge in the Vatican as the Sovereign Military Order of Malta and was headed by a non-voting cardinal and later by Pope Francis as its sovereign head.

The Capitular Commission of surviving Knights of the French Langues reconstituted an English Langue in the 1820s which attracted the attention of the British Royal Family in the 1870s, and later in 1888, Queen Victoria granted it a Royal Charter as an Order of the British Crown.

The Bailiwick of Brandenburg of the German Langue during the Reformation accepted Lutheran theology and maintained connection with their Catholic brethren, recognized the leadership of the grand master of the Order. They paid their dues, but in 1581 the Herrenmeister of the Bailiwick failed to appear before the grand master of the Order, Jean de la Cassiére, and a chapter general of the Catholic Order and the grand master expelled them from the Roman Catholic main stem of the Order.

The Bailiwick, nevertheless, was allowed to pay its dues and by 1641, they were still maintaining connection with their Catholic brethren on Malta. Under the terms of the Peace of Westphalia ending the Thirty Years War between Catholics and Protestants, the Bailiwick was placed under the protection of the prince electors of Brandenburg and later the kings of Prussia with its headquarters at Sonnenburg Castle in the Neumark of Brandenburg.

Despite cordial relations and participation with their German Catholic Knights in a Chapter General of the Order of Malta in 1776, nominal union of the two Orders was prevented by the withholding of papal approval, and in 1784 the Anglo Bavarian Langue with a Polish and a Russian Grand

Priory was established with papal approval.

After the last grand master of the Order on Malta, Ferdinand von Hoempisch zu Bolheim, abdicated on July 6, 1799, a majority of the Order's knights formed a Chapter General, and the knights that had fled to Saint Petersburg elected Czar Paul I as grand master of the Order which was accepted later, grudgingly, by the pope.

Randall had forgotten that the Alsatian Knight of the Order, Baron Johann Baptiste Anton von Flachslanden, was the captain general of the Order's powerful Mediterranean fleet that prowled the sea lanes protecting European merchant shipping from the marauding Muslim pirates who were taking plunder and selling sailors and passengers into slavery.

Flachslanden was also the master of an intricate web of spies maintained by the Order throughout the Muslim world and the Ottoman Empire. He was also the mastermind behind the creation of the Anglo Bavarian Langue in 1784 under the leadership of Grand Master Emmanuel de Rohan Polduc.

Randall remembered that the Baron von Flachslanden and a few of the knights of the Anglo Bavarian Langue had put up a stiff resistance to the landing of Napoleon's forces and that he had barely escaped capture.

Randall pondered the thought, "Maybe since von Flachslanden was a natural leader who had narrowly missed being elected grand master and was the head and creator of the Anglo Bavarian Langue, that maybe, just maybe, he would hurriedly remove the most valuable objects in the Anglo Bavarian Chapel before they were grabbed by Napoleon's army.

"The grail and the skull! Of course! If Napoleon had the grail, it would give him almost mystical power! He could use them as propaganda to make his enemies think he was unbeatable."

Randall snapped his fingers, "That was it. Flachslanden took the only part of the treasure that was invaluable—the cup Jesus had at the Last Supper and the skull that was venerated by the Knights Templar!"

Randall was almost ecstatic about his sudden revelation. He had to talk with Dietrich and Christopher. If they thought it was a good idea, he would contact Dr. Browne's colleagues at the University of Edinburgh Medical School and its genetic research team and see if they could get a carbon date on the bones and teeth to see if the DNA matched any of the DNA that Dr. Tabor and his colleagues discovered from bone fragments left in the ossuaries that were found in the Tomb of the Jesus Family.

He could have Dr. Tabor examine the ossuary and the bones and determine to whom the skeleton and the ossuary belonged.

If Baron von Flachslanden fled for his life with the skull and the grail, he would probably have gone to his home in Bavaria. It seemed to him that he remembered that his old friend, Professor Allen F. Gaw, chairman of the History Department at the University of Texas at the main campus in Austin had mentioned to him long ago that the baron had restored an old Jesuit monastery somewhere in Bavaria. He thought he remembered that Dr. Gaw had said something about Munich. He decided that before he said anything to Natalie, Dietrich, and Christopher he should call Allen and double check the story.

He went immediately to his room at the manor and placed a call to Austin. It was five o'clock in the evening in Scotland, but 11 a.m. in Austin. He thought he might be able to catch him before he went to lunch.

The telephone rang, and a pleasant voice answered, "Dr. Gaw's office, I'm Ellen, his secretary, how may I help you?"

"Hello, Ellen, this is Dr. Randall Fox. Is Dr. Gaw available to speak with me?"

She replied, "Dr. Fox…"

Before she could say anything else, he heard Dr. Gaw's voice in the background repeat his name and then pick up a telephone and say, "Randall, is that you? It's like a voice from the past. Where are you? Are you on one of your digs?"

The words tumbled all over each other without a breath in

between.

"Yes, it's me and I'm not really on a dig."

And then he heard the click of a telephone as Ellen hung up and suddenly Allen's voice continued, "Hey! I just got back from visiting John Valenza, dean at the University of Texas Dental School, and speaking at the Cooley Center in Houston. It's really fabulous.... What's up, where are you?"

"I'm in Inverness, Scotland, and I've got a very important question for you since you are an expert on American and European history in the seventeenth and eighteenth centuries."

"Shoot," he heard Allen quickly reply.

"Do you remember when we were talking about Baron Johann Baptist Anton von Flachslanden and the Order of Saint John when Napoleon attacked the island of Malta?"

"Yes, What about him?"

"Do you remember where the Baron went after he fled the island?"

"Sure, he went to his home in Neuburg outside Munich," replied Allen.

"Tell me about it," Randall continued.

"Well, there's not much to tell. The baron had deposited large sums of money from his former income in British and German banks and then retired to his residence in Neuburg. He had taken a former Jesuit monastery and converted it into a palatial home with huge gardens with Chinese towers, grottoes, and oriental garden villas. It became a meeting place for sophisticated society, and conversations, receptions, and affairs. His small court and his agricultural and economic activities soon made him one of the leading employers in the region. He died in 1823 and was buried in the St. Michael's Church at Ried, a small suburb across the Donau River. His gardens are now known as the English Gardens. Neuburg is framed by numerous mountains in one of the most beautiful areas in Germany. The contemporary librarian in Neuburg, Anton Förch, described Flachslanden as more materialistic than religious.

"He had numerous business dealings with his old friend, the

Ottoman Sultan Selim III, who was an admirer of European culture, the Enlightenment and modernizing his army and navy with the military organization and structure he saw in Europe.

"He had regular correspondence with von Flachslanden, as well as Louis XVI, before the French Revolution and afterwards with the military genius of the Order of Saint John, Baili von Flachslanden. The sultan was also a poet, musician, and composer. He played several instruments and a reed flute. Some of his compositions are still played in the Middle East and his poetry is on the walls of many mosques, including the Blue Mosque and Saint Sophia in old Constantinople."

"Okay, that really helps me," Randall replied. "Would you be interested in flying over here and going to Bavaria with us?"

"Right now?"

"Yeah, if you can break away in the next couple of weeks."

"Let me check my schedule and see. I would love to. Who are us?" laughed Allen.

"Us!" countered Randall includes the queen of England!" There was sudden silence on the telephone and then Allen whispered in disbelief, "The queen of England?"

"Yep," We're after some treasure that was stolen from the United Kingdom and she wants it back."

"I don't remember reading or hearing anything about it in the news," replied Allen.

Randall laughed and then said, "You wouldn't. It was taken in 1572."

There was silence again and then some laughter on the phone. "Well, better later than never, I guess. What is this treasure?"

Randall choked back the words and then he said, "The Holy Grail and maybe the skull of John the Baptist!"

There was more silence on the phone and then Allen laughed and said, "I guess it is worthy of being recovered since everyone's been looking for the Holy Grail for some time now—only a thousand years or so! I'll call you back and let you know if I can be there."

There was more silence and Randall could hear Ellen in the

background telling Allen that she could clear his schedule for a month, but he couldn't leave for a week.

"Ellen has cleared my schedule and I can leave next week. To where do I need to fly?"

Randall relied, "Thanks, old buddy. Inverness, Scotland. Let me know your flights so we can pick you up at the airport."

23 NEUBURG

Randall had entered the Great Room where Dietrich, Christopher, and Anton were at the bar drinking some Glenlivet single malt Scotch. Christopher was drinking it neat while Anton and Dietrich had mixed it with soda. They looked up as he entered the room and motioned for him to join them. He walked over and Christopher handed him a glass half full of Glenlivet, neat.

"Thanks," Randall said, "I needed that. I just got through talking with Dr. Allen Gaw on the phone." He looked at Christopher and continued, "You remember him, don't you?"

"Yes," replied Christopher as he looked at everyone, "He is the history professor, pediatric dentist, and linguist that lives down the street from Carolyn and me at Point Venture on Lake Travis outside Austin. He is medium in stature with slightly graying hair, but he balances that with his quick wit and charming sense of humor. He has the Frank Lloyd House that looks out on the lake at the tip of the peninsula. When will he be joining us for the trip to Neuburg?"

Randall looked up from his drink and said he thought Professor Gaw would be in Scotland within a week. He thought they could make plans to visit Neuburg, and as soon as the professor had arrived, they would be ready to leave immediately. In the meantime, he was sending the ossuary with the bones and the teeth to the University of Edinburg and the genetic research team in the medical school. He had called the team that would arrive in Edinburgh next week to look at the ossuary and take part in the analysis of it and its remains.

They all were relieved that the experts were going to do spectroscopic analysis, carbon dating, and the necessary DNA test panel to see if any of it matched the findings from the specimens analyzed at the time of the finding of the Jesus Family Tomb in the spring of 1980. Later investigations in 2007 included a spectroscopic analysis of the ossuaries, carbon dating of the specimens, the bone specimen analysis for family DNA coding, and the disturbance of the tomb during the time of the first crusades and resealing of the tomb.

The next week passed quickly, Diamond Dave and his wife Debby had left and gone back to Atlanta, and Balthazar had taken command of the entire manor house and become the permanent sleeping buddy for Kira Ann. Carolyn had given up on rousting him out of Kira's bedroom, and he liked to snuggle at Kira's feet and wake her up in the morning just in time for breakfast.

Dr. Gaw was picked up at the Edinburgh airport by James and Hank and driven to MacIntosh Manor. Everyone was happy to see him and he fit right in with the rest of the adventurers.

The team of Edinburg University researchers had completed their analyses. It was their opinion, based on the translation of the markings on the ossuary, the DNA code from the teeth, and from the bones that showed it was an adult male of moderate build who had been beheaded, that the remains were of John, son of Elisabeth and Zechariah and cousin of Jesus!

Because the carbon dating placed the age of the bones from the first century AD it left no doubt in anyone's mind that they were pursuing the skull of John the Baptist, the patron saint of both the Knights Templar and the Hospitaller Order of Saint

John. Sir Richard, upon hearing the results of the bone and ossuary analysis, wrapped an immediate cloud of secrecy around the discoveries.

From this point forward, the pursuit of the grail and skull was in the hands of the MI5 team with Allen, Randall, Christopher, Natalie, and Dietrich. The next week, the team made their plans to go to Neuburg, Germany.

The Neuburg Luftwaffe Air Base, Fliegerhorst Neuburg, was the home of Jagdgeschwader 74, which provides for the air defense of Southern Germany. Since 2006 two squadrons of Eurofighter Typhoons have been operated from the base, and at one time Dietrich had been stationed there. Since he was a pilot and a colonel in the Luftwaffe and knew Neuburg and Lieutenant Colonel Hans Paffenberger, the commander of the airbase very well, he and Betty were able to make the necessary arrangements with the help of MI5 and Sir Richard for them to fly the queen's jet to the base and park it in one of the Luftwaffe hangars. The mission was kept secret because their intention was to fly into the base, proceed to the church in Ried, find Baron von Flachslanden's grave, and see if it would provide any clues for their quest.

Everyone had settled down inside the queen's jet and began talking about what they might find in Neuburg. Dietrich was familiar with Neuburg and knew exactly where the church in Ried where Baron Flachslanden was entombed was located. He had been to the Dom by the Schloss Neuburg as well as the Ried Kirche when he was stationed there.

Christopher and Dietrich went forward into the cockpit to talk with Hank and James who were going to fly them to Neuburg. Because of the military experience Christopher and Dietrich had, they wanted to examine the cockpit of the aircraft. Dietrich said that he liked the layout of the instrumentation and noticed that the aircraft had air defense capability. When he asked Hank and James about that, they explained that the queen's aircraft had been modified and was normally maintained and flown by the RAF when the Royal Family or their guests were on board.

FRANK R. FAUNCE AND JOE C. RUDÉ

He winked at them and whispered, "Since we are on a secret mission, this airplane is officially not here or anywhere that we will be. We are a ghost aircraft that doesn't exist!"

And then they all laughed.

After Christopher and Dietrich returned to their seats, Natalie brought some Glenlivet Scotch, neat of course, with a seltzer chaser and no ice.

Natalie quipped, "We think everyone can handle the drinks. After we are airborne and at our cruising altitude of 25,000 feet, Betty and I have arranged a treat for everyone, thanks to Carolyn."

Christopher smiled and said, "It's got to be her brownies with pecans or her chocolate chip cookies. Right?"

Natalie grinned and replied, "You're only partially correct. You'll just have wait in suspense and guess."

Allen had been patiently observing all of the banter and offered, "Well, I'm just fine with what we have. I remember when Dr. Fox introduced me to Glenlivet years ago."

Natalie smiled and said, "That sounds like him. He loves to check out various kinds of Scotch, I've noticed."

Randall winced and added, "Not just Scotch!" And then he smiled and leaned back in his chair just as Hank appeared from the cockpit.

"Okay, everyone buckle up, we've just been cleared for takeoff," he said and then disappeared back into the cockpit. They were on their way to Neuburg.

Several hours later, they were approaching Neuburg. The sky was clear and the weather perfect. All of the passengers were full and satisfied from the lunch of a mixed salad with vinaigrette dressing, lobster bisque and quiche Loraine, Rhine wine, and topped off with a dessert of Neapolitan ice cream, cookies, brownies, and coffee.

Natalie announced to everyone that she and Rania had made the lobster bisque since Carolyn is allergic to shellfish.

Allen was sleeping quietly and Betty carefully buckled his seatbelt and whispered into his ear, "Dr. Gaw, we are landing at Neuburg," and then she sat down in her seat and buckled

130

her seatbelt.

Allen mumbled, "Okay," and then closed his eyes again.

The jet landed smoothly and then was guided into a hangar which was guarded by Luftwaffe sentries carrying Heckler and Koch MP-5/10 10mm automatic submachine guns.

They all deplaned and were escorted to a waiting silver grey 2017 GLS 550 SUV. Since Dietrich was an active duty colonel in the Luftwaffe on official leave with a military license and credentials, he was allowed to be the designated driver for their expedition to the Ried Kirche. They had left their baggage on the aircraft since they did not know what they would find inside the church where Baron von Flachslanden was entombed. The Luftwaffe was going to refuel their aircraft and have it ready for departure, and Dietrich would give the tower their flight plan after returning.

It took them about an hour to drive through the ancient gate in the medieval wall surrounding the city of Neuburg, past the Castle, Schloss Neuburg on Luitpoldstraße and across the Danube River to the suburb of Ried north of the castle onto Ingolstädter straße, then left onto Eichstätter Straße, past Kirchbergstraße to the church with its's bell tower. It was on the left side of the street tucked back from it.

They turned into the church parking lot and parked the car. There was still sunlight with just a few puffy white clouds catching the sunlight of the waning day and giving them a slight pink tinge. They all scrambled out of their car and saw that a priest was waiting for them. He politely opened the entrance door to the church and led them down the aisle to the altar. Off to the left was an elaborate tombstone in the floor covering the sarcophagus of the Baron von Flachslanden.

They looked with amazement at the ornate tombstone and they saw the now familiar chevron with the small circle under the point of the chevron. But there was something else they had not seen before—the image of a skull but no crossbones. Where the crossbones would normally be was the Latin phrase, "Respice in sancta sapientia corum VXLV," and underneath, chiseled in German, was a prayer.

Allen kneeled down and then took out a folding magnifying glass that he used to examine old manuscripts and pronounced, "There is a very thin horizontal bar chiseled over the V! What do you make of that?"

Dietrich and Randall took a picture of the tombstone. Dietrich translated the prayer into English for everyone. The prayer was simple, but enigmatic.

He read, "With God's mercy, look to the heavens for salvation and the Holy of God at the altar of Faith and Wisdom. Put your heart at rest and drink from the Cup of Forgiveness of all Sins for its Grace has returned."

They stared at the prayer which was almost a poem of spiritual guidance.

Allen got down on one knee and carefully examined the engraved words, then he said, "This is a code and I think it might be a Merkebah Substitution Cipher."

Randall looked at his old friend and said, "Yes, I think I remember what Dr. James Schonfield said about it."

Then he looked at Dietrich, smiled, and quipped, "I believe Dr. Schonfield might also be a cousin of yours. He wrote the book, *Merkabah Mysticism,* in which he says that a system of cryptology called the Merkabah ciphers had been used to conceal certain names in Essene, Zadokite, and Nazarene texts found in a number of the Qumran scrolls."

He said, "By applying the Hebrew Merkabah code to the prayer, it could refer to the Holy Grail. Therefore, what the Templars really worshipped with a skull was really the principle of the wisdom espoused by John the Baptist. The Templars, in their reverence of the Sacred Feminine of the heretical Cathars and their rule which was written by Saint Bernard who was obsessed with *The Song of Solomon* and their code of extreme courtesy toward females was also expressed by their worship of the Virgin Mary as well as Mary Magdalene. This is seen in their chapels such as Saint Mary in Scotland south of Rosslyn Chapel in Scotland.

"Remember in the Gospel of Philip in the heretical gnostic Nag Hammadi scrolls found in Egypt, it said that Mary

Magdalene was the one who would carry his church forward and she was his favorite among the apostles and loved her more than them and would kiss her on the…, but that part of the parchment was missing.

"That is why many of the cathedrals and chapels in Europe built by the Cistercians, an order closely aligned with the Templars, many of whom were Cathars, had a rose window above the altar facing east to catch the image of Venus, which is significant for the Sacred Feminine. Venus was also used for the time for the planting of crops in the Mother Earth in the spring and the reaping of the harvest in the fall. Venus rises in the east in the morning during spring at the time of planting and rises in the west in the evening during fall at the time of harvesting."

Natalie had been listening to this exchange and proffered the possibility that the verse might be referring to a place, "We might be trying to complicate things."

Allen looked up with a jerk of his head and said, "Yes, you just might be right. Sometimes things are so simple, it might be hidden in plain sight."

Randall looked at everyone and said, "You know, I have a friend who has lived in the Middle East and Europe and is proficient in medieval history and Latin. Allen, you might know him. He is a professor at the University of North Carolina, Dr. Peter Hawkins. Let me call him and ask what he thinks about what we have found."

Allen said that he knew of him, but they had not met. They all nodded their approval of the suggestion and Randall flipped through his contacts and found Dr. Hawkins' office number. He pressed the call button and soon heard a soft voice announce that her name was Teresa, Dr. Hawkins' secretary.

"May I speak to Dr. Hawkins? My name is Dr. Randall Fox and we are old friends."

"Oh, Dr. Fox, yes. Dr. Hawkins has spoken frequently of you. Dr. Hawkins is not here. He is in Istanbul on a research trip and I know he would be delighted to speak with you. Do you have his cell phone number?"

"Yes, I do. Thank you so much for your kindness and courtesy. I know that Dr. Hawkins always has the best people working with him and I'm sure that if you are as beautiful as your voice, then he is doubly blessed. Thank you."

There was a moment of silence followed by a soft giggle and then Teresa said, "Dr. Hawkins always said that you are kind. Come visit with us sometime." And then she giggled and said, "Goodbye."

Randall hung up the telephone and started to call Dr. Hawkins' cell phone.

Christopher motioned to Randall and remarked, "Randall, that is a side of you that I have never fully appreciated."

Randall smiled and then called Dr. Hawkins' cell phone.

The telephone rang a couple of times and then the familiar voice of Dr. Hawkins answered, "Randall, is that you? What's up?"

"I'm in Germany at Baron von Flachslanden's tomb and I need your help."

"Sure, what do you need?"

"Well, I've got this poem on a tombstone that I believe is a puzzle or a cipher. There is a Latin phrase above it with the Latin number VXLV with a horizontal bar over the first V."

Randall recited the poem, and when Dr. Hawkins repeated it, he laughed and said, "Oh, 6,045 is the Byzantine calendar date for the dedication of the Hagia Sophia here in Istanbul. It is about the only event of note in history that year. History scholars convert 6,045 Anno Mundi, which is Latin for 'in the year of the world,' to 537 Anno Domini 'in the year of our Lord,' when writing for the public. Also, the full name of the Hagia Sophia in English is 'Shrine of the Holy of God.' So your poem is a subtle reference to Hagia Sophia as well.

"The poem also sounds like something that Sultan Selim III would have written. Sultan Selim III would have used the Byzantine calendar for his business, and Baron Flachslanden, as a close friend, would know this. He would know that someone would have to be familiar with Byzantine culture to recognize it as a date in the Byzantine calendar system as well as a pointer to the Ottomans.

"In fact, given that Baron Flachslanden was the spymaster for the Hospitaller Order of Saint John and with his business relationships with the sultan, he would had to have a working knowledge of their calendar system since he would have had to convert dates back and forth in the Julian calendar.

"Sultan Selim III had some of his poems placed in several mosques like the Blue Mosque here in Istanbul and maybe also in the Hagia Sophia.

"What's going on, old buddy? Sounds like something big."

Randall laughed and then coyly whispered, "It involves the queen of England."

There was silence for a few seconds and Randall began to worry that they had been disconnected when a whisper from Peter slowly emanated from the phone, "Wow, you aren't kidding. When will you be here?"

"Right away and I'm bringing some friends and a team of MI5 people and the queen's jet with me!"

More silence and then Peter said, "Sounds good, can hardly wait. Okay!"

"I'll be back in touch and let you know when. Okay?"

And then they hung up.

Everyone had been listening to the conversation on speaker and they were also speechless at what had just transpired.

The silence was broken when Natalie quipped, "See, I told you it was something simple and hiding in plain sight."

Everyone laughed and then Natalie turned to Allen and asked, "Would you tell me what this Hagia Sophia is and what it's all about?"

Allen took a deep breath and said, "It's the oldest cathedral in Christendom. It was started by Constantine and finished in its present form in 537 AD by the Byzantine Roman Emperor Justinian I. It was sacked by the crusaders during the Fourth Crusade when Constantinople was captured in 1204.

"It was occupied by the Catholics until its recapture by the Greek Orthodox Byzantines in 1261. In May of 1453, Constantinople was captured by the Ottoman Turks who turned it into a mosque and placed four minarets around it. After that it was and is still known as the Hagia Sophia. In 1935, the first Turkish president of the Turkish Republic, Mustafa Kemal Atatürk, turned it and the Topkapi Palace of the Sultans into museums run by the Turkish Ministry of Culture."

The statute was created as a result of pressure from Christians and Muslims to turn the Hagia Sophia into their respective religion's holy place. So Atatürk chose a middle ground and turned the Hagia Sophia and the Topkapi Place into museums for everyone.

Randall listened and remarked, "Natalie is correct. We are trying to make this complicated when it is really quite simple. Baron Johann Baptist Anton von Flachslanden missed by only a couple of votes in 1797 by the Chapter General of becoming the grand master of the Hospitaller Order of Saint John on Malta. He was also the grand prior of the Anglo Bavarian Langue, a close friend of Czar Paul I, but—get this—he was also a really close friend of Sultan Selim III who was a poet, musician, and artist who greatly admired European culture. He also had his lyrics and poems placed on enameled mosaics in several mosques such as the Blue Mosque in Constantinople, or Istanbul as it's known today!"

Natalie coolly said, "Could this poem have been written by Sultan Selim III?"

Allen said, "Yes, it sounds very much like something he would have written. I understand the various dialects of the Arabic language and instead of the word God, he would have used Allah."

Christopher was earnestly listening to the conversation and exclaimed, "I believe we need to fly to Istanbul. Is that possible, if we get right back to the airplane?"

Dietrich looked around at everyone and replied, "Everyone game for a night flight to Istanbul?"

24 ISTANBUL

The flight was finally cleared by eight o'clock that evening and everyone had declined to eat their dinner in Neuburg. Instead, the commander of the Fliegerhorst Neuburg, Lt. Col. Paffenberger had a dinner of sauerkraut and bratwurst and wiener schnitzel with kopfsalat with a sweetened vinaigrette, potato salad and cucumbers, a dessert of apfel pie with vanilla ice cream, and of course, some Von Trapp Dunkel lager beer delivered to their airplane.

The queen's jet cleared the runway and rapidly gained altitude as they headed for Istanbul. They were cleared for an altitude of 25,000 feet and after a few hours were heading into the morning sky and the breaking dawn. They were almost to Istanbul and all of the passengers, including Betty, were still fast asleep.

Hank and James were in the cockpit waiting for landing instructions from the Istanbul Atatürk Airport control tower. After a half-hour wait and circling one of the busiest airports in the Middle East, they finally received the authorization to land and taxi to a military hangar where they would be met by a special envoy from the British Embassy.

Atatürk Airport is on the European side of Istanbul 15

miles west of the city's center and their destination in the old city. The approach to the airfield is from the southwest over the water of the Marmara Sea.

Hank quietly slipped back into the passenger cabin to awaken Betty, but he found her looking out her window. He tapped her on the shoulder and she looked up. "Yeah, I know, it's time for everyone to get ready to land, deplane, and get to our hotel."

Their hotel was the Magnaura Palace Hotel in the heart of Istanbul, only 800 feet from the Hagia Sophia. The hotel was picked not only because of its proximity to the subject of their quest, but also because of its luxurious suites with a terrace that overlooks the Bosphorus and the Marmara Sea, and more importantly, wonderful showers.

Betty and Hank woke everyone up, but had a little difficulty with Dr. Gaw, who had not completely adjusted to the time difference between Europe, Turkey, and Austin, Texas. When he finally opened his eyes and looked out his window, the jet was a few inches over the concrete airstrip, just about to touch down.

There was a sudden shudder in the aircraft as it touched down and quickly moved to the Turkish military hangar and their waiting envoy.

As soon as they stopped inside the hangar, Hank and James opened the aircraft's door and deployed the ladder to the ground.

Everyone deplaned and an embassy van was there to transport them to their hotel. Their rooms were ready when they finally arrived. The British Embassy had already checked them in under diplomatic coverage and fictitious names. They were issued their new passports with diplomatic immunity and they were advised to keep a low profile and that MI5 would be looking over their shoulders while they were in Istanbul.

There had been some recent terrorist attacks and they weren't going to take any chances. Everyone had activated their signet rings and were now being monitored by Kate and Steve at MacIntosh Manor. Kira had wanted to send a message to her parents, but Steve had explained that her parents would be out of touch for the next few days. She didn't quite understand, but accepted Uncle Steve's suggestion.

Allen was fascinated by the signet ring he had been issued and very quickly picked up the nuances of its operation.

Betty had contacted the British Embassy in Ankara and they arranged for Dr. Peter Hawkins to meet them at ten o'clock the next morning at the entrance to the Hagia Sophia.

Hank and James were exhausted and said they were going to catch a few "Zs" and would be available for dinner. Everyone else was anxious to take a refreshing shower and get dressed for a hearty breakfast on the terrace.

After breakfast, they walked through the park with its reflecting pool and large fountain, to the entrance of the Hagia Sophia and saw the smiling face of Dr. Peter Hawkins. He was about six feet tall with blond hair and sparkling blue eyes. His grin was wide, revealing perfect teeth. He was lean with just a little bit of age creeping up on the fiftyish professor. He was standing erect with a military bearing, waving some tickets in the air. He had already bought tickets for everyone and they entered the Hagia Sophia.

They were astounded at the immensity of the structure which had been built with the skill of the ancient Roman and Byzantine world. The once-cathedral has a gigantic dome in the center of the north-south oriented nave which is 182 feet high and approximately 110 feet in diameter. The nave was actually aligned more southwest so it pointed toward Jerusalem. The apses on the north and south sides of the semicircular vaulted nave were smaller half domes that were smaller, but nevertheless equally impressive.

Numerous chandeliers were hanging by chains from the ceiling of the nave, giving additional light to the interior of the structure. There were stained glass windows at the ends and sides of the apses. There were numerous windows around the base of the central dome giving it the impression of floating in space. The dome at the center had a painting of the sun with rays of light radiating from it down the dome's structural ribbing, making it appear like rays from the sun. It was very reminiscent of ancient Egyptian paintings of Ra, the sun god, during the time of Akhenaten and Nefertiti.

There were many windows around the second floor and third floor galleries admitting light to reveal the myriad of paintings and mosaics decorating the walls, columns, and pillars. The south apse had once held the altar of the Hagia Sophia when it was a Christian cathedral called the Cathedral of Saint Sophia. In the sixteenth century, the Sultan Suleiman the Magnificent (1520-1566) brought back two colossal candlesticks from his conquest of Hungary. They were placed on either side of the mihrab which is located in the south apse where the altar used to stand. The mihrab was slightly off center and pointed toward Mecca. The altar and the apse pointed toward Jerusalem.

Above the beautiful stained glass windows at the gallery level above the mihrab was the Virgin and Child mosaic which was the first of the post-iconoclastic mosaics. It was inaugurated on March 29, 867, by Patriarch Photius and the emperors Michael III and Basil I. This mosaic was located in a high location on the half dome of the apse. Mary was sitting on a throne without a back holding the Christ Child on her lap. Her feet rested on a pedestal and the throne and pedestal were adorned with precious stones. The portrait paintings of the archangels Michael and Gabriel are in the bema of the arch and are very faint.

At the northern end of the nave was another half domed apse with stained glass windows and other windows at the gallery level to illuminate the apse. There were also large round black signs at the gallery level hung on the railings of the second level gallery proclaiming in Arabic script that God is great.

The Deësis mosaic was probably done in 1261 at the end of the 57 years of Roman Catholic use and then returned to the Orthodox faith. It was the third panel situated in the imperial enclosure of the upper galleries.

Peter had led the way and proceeded to point out and

explain all the nuances of the former Saint Sophia Cathedral and its mosaics and their history. He and Allen were discussing also the Muslim mosaics when Allen mentioned Sultan Selim III and asked if he had any of his work in the Hagia Sophia.

Peter replied, "Yes, there were several."

Peter asked Allen if there was any one of his sayings or poems he was referring to.

"Not really, but I'll know it when I see it."

They, along with Christopher, Natalie, and Dietrich who were walking with Betty after peering through all of the galleries on the second and third levels, were now roaming the lower level and walking toward the south apse.

Suddenly Allen stopped and snapped his fingers. "Hey, did everyone notice how the Deësis Mosaic in the third panel of the imperial enclosure of the upper galleries where the Virgin Mary and John the Baptist are imploring the intercession of Christ for humanity on Judgement Day."

They all looked at him and Dietrich said, "Yeah, what are you driving at?"

Allen replied, "What was it that was written on Baron Flachslanden's tombstone? Didn't it say, 'Put your heart at rest and drink from the cup of forgiveness of all sins for its Grace has returned?' Doesn't that mean the intercession of Christ for humanity at Judgement Day?"

"Yeah, I suppose," said Peter.

"Did you notice that John the Baptist and the Virgin Mary were looking toward the south apse and the figure of the Christ Child and the Virgin Mary?"

Natalie chimed in, "So what does that mean?"

Allen continued, "It means that the next part of the clue is located in the south apse. Remember when Randall and Peter were talking about the possibility that the inscription on Baron Flachslanden's tombstone was written by Selim III and that he put mosaics of his writings in various mosques?"

Peter picked up on what Allen was saying, "Yes, just suppose that writing on Flachslanden's tombstone you saw is also on some mosaic in the south apse of the Hagia Sophia.

Let's go over there and look for it."

Randall blurted, "But the mosaic won't be in German. It will be in Arabic and we can't read it, let alone speak it. I wish Rania was here."

Allen and Peter looked at each other and both smiled as they threw both of their arms into the air and simultaneously said, "We can read and speak it!"

Randall half muttered under his breath, "I should have known that. Both of you understand more languages than anyone else I know."

Allen winked at his friends and said, "Even Mandarin Chinese."

Allen elaborated, "Well I should. My parents were born in China. I even know some of the American Indian lingo." And then he laughed, "Come on, let's go see what we can find."

They all followed behind Allen and Peter who had taken the lead toward the south apse. Allen and Peter walked over to the stairway to the pulpit and stairs on the right side of the apse and they all followed them as they started to circumnavigate the apse. About a quarter way around the apse, Peter suddenly stopped in front of a mosaic and started to read it.

He read, "With Allah's mercy, look to the heavens for the Holy of Allah and put your heart at rest and drink from the cup of forgiveness of all sins for its Grace has returned."

They all gasped when Allen then pointed out the chevron arch with a small circle beneath the point just above the writing. Peter, Allen, Betty and Randall all took pictures of the written mosaic with the chevron and circle. Then, they looked at the mosaic of the Virgin with the Christ Child on her lap and took pictures of that mosaic with their iPhone cameras.

After taking their pictures, Peter followed the writings advice and looked up. All he could see was the colored light from the stained glass windows streaming through them, and there shimmering in the light was the illumination of the Christ Child with his round head circumscribed by a unique tri-radiant halo whose three rays created a chevron. He was sitting in the lap of his mother Mary pointing south by southwest toward

Jerusalem.

"That's it," stammered Peter. "The baron got permission from Selim III to return the skull and the grail to the place the Templars originally found them in the time after the First Crusade when they broke into the Tomb of the Jesus Family in Talpiot between Bethlehem and Jerusalem. The clues all point to Jerusalem as the place we can find and recover the Holy Grail and the partial skull of John the Baptist and reunite it with the rest of his bones."

They all sighed, and Betty looked at everyone and said, "Well let's all go back to the hotel, wake up Hank and James, have a good dinner, celebrate the last leg of our journey of discovery, and at least get a good night's rest before we fly down to Jerusalem tomorrow. I have a few things to do."

She looked up at Peter and exclaimed, "You have no idea what a valuable contribution you have made to humanity. It's scientists like you, Allen, and Randall who evaporate ignorance for wisdom. You will join us for dinner won't you?"

Peter replied, "You are most gracious. I will. What time"

"About eight."

She realized that Sir Richard would have to pull a few strings to allow them to nose around Jerusalem trying to recover items stolen long ago from the United Kingdom. Even longer ago, the Knights Templar stole from what is now Israel, whose rights have precedent in a case that spans a thousand or even two thousand years.

Anyway, she was going to do her job and report their findings and just let Sir Richard and the queen ponder the long-range question of ownership.

Everyone seemed pleased with what they had discovered, and Peter, Allen, and Randall were thinking of how to present their findings to the scientific community and to the administrations of the University of Texas and the University of North Carolina who employed them.

As they started to trudge out of the Hagia Sophia, no one had noticed two men dressed in typical Saudi Arabian white robed thobes, Bisht and red checkered Ghutra and Egal that had been watching them as they had wandered through the Hagia Sophia. They had been taking pictures of them and when Betty and her team left the Hagia Sophia Museum, they walked over to the mosaic with the writing and the chevron and circle they had found and took pictures of it and then looked up and took pictures of the apse image of the Virgin with the Christ Child on her lap.

25 JERUSALEM

Hank and James were still asleep in their rooms at the Magnaura Palace Hotel when Betty and her five wards returned to the hotel. They had all gone back to their rooms with the understanding that they would get together later with Peter, Randall, Allen, and Christopher. They were all sharing a large suite with a large terrace overlooking the Marmara Sea, and Peter joined them.

Randall had already arranged for a couple of bottles of Glenlivet and Lismore single malt scotch with an appropriate number of glasses and bottled seltzer—no ice with an appropriate selection of hors d'oeuvres, pretzels, and some sort of a chip that resembled potato chips with an onion dip.

They had all agreed that they would not drink too much Scotch since a good bottle of Dom Perignon 1990 champagne would be appropriate for the evening meal before their departure for Jerusalem the next day. Betty had already called and talked with Sir Richard and checked with the British Embassy for their departure the next morning at eleven o'clock. The fight to Jerusalem would not take long and the British Embassy there was already making arrangements for them to stay in four suites at the King David Jerusalem Hotel, which would be close by where they wanted to go.

Eight o'clock soon rolled around and everyone met and went downstairs to the restaurant for a farewell dinner with shish kebab as the main course. A lobster bisque soup with a green garden salad were served with mineral water and a Dom Perignon 1990 champagne followed by the main course. Then chocolate mousse for dessert with Napoleon brandy or Grand Marnier liqueur with dark coffee were served with cream on the side.

After dinner, everyone said farewell to Peter for his assistance and assured him that they would let him know what happened in Jerusalem.

The next morning, everyone had breakfast in their rooms and met downstairs at eight o'clock for their trip to the Atatürk Airport and the hangar where the queen's jet was parked. After they boarded and took their seats, Hank announced that they had been given clearance to take off on the short runway and would again be cruising at 25,000 feet to Jerusalem.

The flight went smoothly and soon they were in a landing pattern over Ben Gurion International Airport. It is located 12 miles to the southeast of Tel Aviv and is considered to be among the five best airports in the Middle East. They were soon on the ground and directed to an Israeli Defense Force military hangar where they were met by an IDF team and a member of MI5 from the British Embassy with a van to take them the 34 miles to Jerusalem. Normally at this time it would take about 45 minutes to an hour to get to the King David Hotel, but the traffic was unusually heavy for this time of day.

When they finally arrived an hour and fifteen minutes later, everyone was a little tired and since they were already checked in, it took hardly any time for them and their baggage to arrive in their suites.

They had planned to visit the Israel Antiquities Authority and their warehouse in Bet Shemesh and talk with members of their staff about the Jesus Family Tomb in East Talpiot and the ossuary exhibits in the Israeli Museum and the Rockefeller Museum where the Israeli Antiquities Authority was originally housed on the morning of Friday, March 18, 1980, when the Talpiot Tomb was discovered.

The British Embassy had anticipated the late arrival and had arranged for them to visit the Israeli Antiquities Authority the next morning. For the time being they were on their own, so they decided to meet in Christopher's suite to have some Scotch and hors d'oeuvres and discuss what they should do for the rest of the day.

After refreshing themselves, they all arrived in Christopher's suite where the hors d'oeuvres, Chardonnay and Merlot wines with Glenlivet Scotch and soda with plates and glasses, had already arrived and were laid out in splendid fashion on the table in the dining room off the sitting room.

Natalie and Dietrich were the first to arrive. Natalie looked wonderful in a light yellow dress with a short white jacket. Her long dark hair hung like a halo around her shoulders and bounced when she walked. She had decided on low heeled brown leather walking shoes for any excursion into the old city they might experience.

Betty was dressed in light blue frilly summer dress without sleeves, and a white silk scarf was wrapped off center around her shoulders. Her hair, which she usually wore in a bun, was now loose and cascaded in curls down her back and shoulders. She also wore low heeled light brown shoes.

Allen remarked, "Wow, you're going to turn some heads if we go for a walk in the old town."

Betty blushed and then Natalie remarked about Betty, "She would turn heads if she were dressed in anything. She's beautiful regardless of any kind of dress."

Everyone smiled.

Allen turned red and said, "I know that, I just meant she looked exceptionally beautiful tonight."

Betty turned to Allen and said, "Well thank you sir. I appreciate your remarks and know you were just trying to be complimentary."

They then proceeded to get a plate and take whatever hors d'oeuvres they wanted along with an appropriate drink, and go outside onto the patio.

Natalie walked over to Betty and Allen and said, "You know, these last few days have been tiring. Why don't we just have a light dinner served here tonight after our walk in the old city? Then we'll feel better in the morning for our trip to the IAA."

Betty agreed and said to everyone, "I've been talking with Natalie and Allen and we believe that all of us would feel better if we just had dinner here and enjoyed each other's company today without an agenda. What do you all think?"

Christopher smiled, winked at Allen and Randall, turned to Betty and said, "Now, y'all are talking like a Texan!"

No one knew that the party on the patio was being watched by two men with black hair and swarthy complexions with binoculars from a neighboring building. One of them remarked to the other, "Are you sure they are going to be at the IAA tomorrow morning?"

"Yes, our contact inside the IAA is definite on that point. This matter concerns the queen of England herself!"

The next morning they all met in the hotel's King's Garden Restaurant for a Mediterranean breakfast of fresh fruits, orange juice, and eggs benedict with strawberries, served with dark coffee and cream. Christopher and Allen decided on waffles with butter and honey served with coffee and cream.

After breakfast they were picked up in front of the hotel by a van from the British Embassy and taken to the Israeli Antiquities Authority and its warehouse in Bet Shemesh. They arrived at their destination shortly after and were met at the entrance by the director of the Antiquities Authority. A pleasant secretary showed the way to a boardroom with a large walnut conference table and chairs where they were directed to take their places around it. Soon the young lady came back into the room with cups, glasses, napkins, spoons, a pitcher of dark coffee, cream and sugar, and a pitcher of fresh spring water.

The director pleasantly said, "I've been advised by your Sir Richard that you are looking for some answers to a quest you are engaged in. It may take a few minutes, but I believe we have someone here that can give you most of the answers you're seeking. There is some good news and some not so good news. Let me give you the good news first. I know you're seeking the Holy Grail and the good news is that we have it and it is secure!"

A ripple of sighs of relief circled the conference table.

"The bad news is that the skull of John the Baptist is gone forever. Let me clarify that—we do have it, but it is gone forever. I have one of the archeologists from our Antiquities Authority who will explain it more thoroughly. Let me introduce you to Dr. Avrim Levitus and I'll let him explain."

Dr. Levitus was an older man with greying hair and an infectious smile He was about five feet ten inches in stature, a slight pot belly, and was wearing a sport coat and tie with patches on the elbows. As he rose from his seat at the table, he took a remote device from his pocket to operate his LCD PowerPoint projector to demonstrate with photos, video, and sketches what he was going to present to the group.

"Good morning, I don't want to bore you or take up your time with excuses about the technology we have today, but did not have in 1980 when our story all began. It all began with an excavation in East Talpiot on the Bethlehem Road in the spring of 1980.

"If it had not been for the quick action of a neighborhood mother, Rivka Maoz and a couple of history minded engineers including Efraim Schochat who had been directing the bulldozers, the tomb would have been bulldozed into oblivion. Then the world would never have known about the Jesus Family Tomb and its contents or the small stone cup and dishes on a table in the anteroom of the tomb representing the last supper that had spurred so much attention over the centuries.

"The patio where a couple of skeletons were found and the anteroom had been partially demolished by a bulldozer that was ready to smash into the ornately carved large tomb. The tomb had a chevron over a circle at the entrance where a stone door was slightly open as if not closed completely in some past bygone century. The partially destroyed anteroom with the table where a skull, one stone cup, some baskets of dried fruit and bread, and some dishes laid upon it were still evident.

"Ephraim Schochat quickly shouted and stopped the bulldozer from moving forward and causing more damage. He promptly called the Antiquities Authorities and they closed the site until their archeologists could examine, document, and save whatever antiquities and artifacts for posterity. It was late in the afternoon and too late for the archeologists to arrive that day. They would arrive early the following morning.

"The small stone cup that Baron Flachslanden—yes, we know all about your expedition and what you have discovered about how Baron Flachslanden had returned the items in the early 1800s after their long journey from the hidden room under Saint Mary Chapel in Scotland. We now realize the significance of the cup and the skull that the baron had placed on that table. The small stone cup and the skull were picked up the next morning, photographed, catalogued, and labeled before they were carefully packed into small brown boxes, labeled, and sent with the rest of the skeletons and ossuaries to the Antiquities Department in the Rockefeller Museum.

"A skull that had been kicked and partially shattered by a young neighborhood boy and his two playmates pretending it was a soccer ball before they were driven off by Rivka Maoz lay on the ground with some other bones.

"After the boys scattered, she carefully picked up the shattered parts of the skull placed them and the other scattered bones into a black plastic bag. The other bones also had been scattered by the bulldozer and when she and her husband finished picking them up, they filled two bags which she placed for safekeeping into their basement for our antiquities experts who arrived the next morning to preserve and document the contents of the tomb. She and her family kept watch over this important tomb all night to prevent children, grave robbers, and antiquities dealers from stealing them for sale on the Black Market.

"The next morning, our archeologists arrived and she gave

her two bags of bones and skulls to Amos Kloner, a young graduate PhD student archeologist, and Yosef Gat, his supervisor. A young student Amed Shimon Gibson was assigned to sketch the tomb and precisely map the structural detail and contents inside the tomb including all the chambers and ossuaries inside its chambers.

"The tomb had six niches containing ten ossuaries. Five of these niches had five seal stones removed, and clearly, someone centuries before, around the time of the First Crusade, had entered the tomb before the red terra rosa silt had partially filled the tomb and overflowed the ossuaries with red mud. Obviously, someone had entered the tomb centuries before the flow of terra rosa into the tomb. But the ossuaries were undamaged with their lids and contents securely in place as if the intruders were not interested in looting or vandalism.

"When all of the red soil that had flowed into the tomb over the centuries was carefully removed, three skulls forming a perfect triangle on the floor of the tomb were found as if some sort of ritual had been performed at the time of the break-in before the red silt had flowed around the partially closed stone door."

As Dr. Levitus was speaking he was showing the pictures of the tomb and the archeologists' activities, photos, video, and sketches.

"It was later determined that the entry date for the intruders would have been right after the First Crusade when the Knights Templar had arrived in the Holy Land and Jerusalem one thousand years ago!"

"Could this be the time," Dr. Levitus proffered, "that the sealing stones of five of the six niches had been opened until they found the one ossuary they wanted—John the Baptist?

"Could the three skulls found on the floor and carefully documented only to be put in plastic bags to join the rest of the contents of the other ossuaries been the skulls of occupants of three of the recovered ossuaries? And if so which three?

"Could the intruders have been the Knights Templar, and why are the skulls in a triangle? These were all questions that ran through the minds of our antiquities archeologists.

"We would not have known the full story about the tomb and the ten ossuaries if it weren't for Simcha Jacobovici, a Canadian filmmaker who wanted permission to visit the apartment complex that had been built over the tomb and was catalogued as 'IAA 80/500-509.'

"There had been ten ossuaries that were photographed and documented, but one of them disappeared on the way back to the Antiquities Department housed at the Rockefeller Museum at that time. It later turned up being sold to an antique dealer, and the name on the ossuary was 'James, son of Joseph, brother of Jesus.' Other ossuaries had Jesus Family names such as Mariamne, which has been identified with the Greek name Mariamme, from the church Father Origen who calls Mary Magdalene 'Mariamme, the writer Epiphanus, and the Pistia Sophia and the Acts of Philip that identify Mary of Magdalen as Mariamme.

"Other ossuaries carry the names Maria, 'Jesus, son of Joseph,' Matthew, and 'Yosa (nickname for Joseph) brothers of Jesus.' The inscription on another ossuary reads 'Judah, son of Jesus!'

"We did not realize the gravity of the discovery and how it might affect various people, governments, and institutions of the three monotheistic religions involved in this narrative. The tomb still exists, but is now a reliquary for old religious Jewish documents, religious writings, and books. The bones, skulls, and contents of the ossuaries have been collectively buried with orthodox Jewish services into a mass grave whose location I cannot reveal to anyone. I understand that John the Baptist's skeleton without his head and his ossuary is currently being held by the Antiquities Department of Edinburgh University in Edinburgh. We are currently discussing this with the British government."

Dr. Levitus paused and took a drink of water, then he continued, "A condominium apartment complex now resides over the site of the Jesus Family Tomb. A concrete slab in a rose garden next to the complex covers the iron spiral stair steps to the tomb's entrance with its strange chevron and circle.

"It has been postulated by many researchers of antiquities and biblical scholars that the symbol of the chevron and circle goes all the way back to Akhenaten and Nefertiti, Ra, the all seeing eye of God in a triangle and the Sacred Feminine of Isis, Judaism, the Pythagoreans, to early Ebionite Jewish Christians of the first century, the Essenes, the Gnostics, Eastern and Western Christianity, early Islam, the Cathars, Knights Templar, Knights Hospitaller, Frére Maçon, the Enlightenment, the Reformation, and now the Masonic Orders of the present age.

"This secret symbol of a chevron or a triangle with a circle in various forms has existed through the centuries representing the creative force of the universe and monotheism with its Sacred Feminine. And it is even seen on the unfinished pyramid on the back of the United States dollar bill. I hope that this little presentation with the illustrations has given you some satisfaction in the time and labor and dangers to your lives that you have all endured, but we felt you should know everything we know about this situation.

"Are there any questions?"

Everyone around the table was mute. They suddenly realized that their quest and adventures had run their full course. Many questions asked over the ages were beginning to be understood, thanks to the wisdom and technology that was not available in 1980.

Allen raised his hand and asked, "Will we be able to see the Holy Grail and the ossuaries?"

Dr. Levitus replied, "Yes, we had anticipated that and, except for two ossuaries that we have on loan to different museums, we can fulfill your wish. We have some white gloves for everyone and now we'll go to the warehouse where they are kept."

Everyone stood up and followed Dr. Levitus out of the room and down a long hall to the climate-controlled warehouse.

When they entered, Allen leaned over to Christopher and whispered in his ear, "This is just like Indiana Jones and the Lost Ark isn't it?"

Christopher smiled and then replied, "Except this is real!"

26 THE ROSE GARDEN

The team of adventurers had gathered back in Christopher's suite and had migrated to the patio when Randall remarked for all to hear, "I can't believe that we have all held the cup of Christ and have seen his ossuary."

Dietrich added, "I can't believe we have seen the whole family's ossuaries with the exception of James and Matthew."

Betty exclaimed, "Well at least we can say that we have seen John the Baptist's skeleton and ossuary and they haven't."

Natalie replied, "Not yet!"

Randall postulated, "Do you think there might be some DNA on that rough stone cup? You know they can get DNA from saliva and fingerprints now—maybe in the future from just your breath!"

Everyone thought for a few seconds and then burst out in laughter.

The two Arab men watching them through binoculars said, "They are laughing about something. What do you suppose it is?"

Just about that time, his iPhone rang. The voice on the other end said, "Our contact said they are going to be in the rose garden tomorrow afternoon at three o'clock."

The man with the binoculars murmured, "We'll see who has the last laugh."

The next morning everyone had gotten up feeling chipper. Natalie and Dietrich felt good about the results of their little caper. They had gone to bed the night before and dissolved into each other's arms.

Natalie had kissed him on his cheek and whispered into his ear, "How about giving Kira a little brother?"

And then she snuggled close to Dietrich and they made love—it seemed like all night.

After breakfast they all decided to roam around the Old Town of Jerusalem and then get back to their hotel in time to be picked up by a van from the Israeli Antiquities Authority and go to East Talpiot and the rose garden. They didn't know that the two Arab men who had been watching them had arrived at the apartment early that morning before the sun came up.

They had entered in the apartment after rendering the alarm system useless and picking the 1980s style lock. The husband of Adina Chava was away on business, leaving her alone with her five-year-old daughter Dinah and four-year-old son Ariel. They were fast asleep when the men came through the door with two suicide vests and a denim sack filled with C-4 plastic explosive with a detonator button and remote cell phone detonator attached to the side of the bag. Between the vests and the bag there was enough force to bring down the whole apartment building and blast a hole in the rose garden that would totally destroy the Jesus Family Tomb with its symbol of creation and life.

They explained to Adina that she should explain to her children when they woke up that they were cousins who were there for the day and that they were to play in their rooms or watch television since mommy wasn't feeling very well.

After the children woke up, she told them the story the intruders compelled her to tell. She then fixed breakfast for everyone, including the two assassins who projected familiarity, friendliness, and good will in their behavior that was the antithesis of their hearts.

The day progressed until they heard some chatter and noise as Betty and her wards came down the concrete stairs to the patio and rose garden in front of Adina's apartment. The older man who had been watching with binoculars the day before put his finger in front of his lips to signal silence to Adina and her children and to sit on the couch and watch television with their mother. Then he and his younger disciple put on their suicide vests.

Ariel looked at the two men and asked his mother quietly, "Why are they putting on those vests? It's warm today."

The older man put his finger to his lips and looked sternly at Ariel who then shrank down and put his arms around his mother.

Betty and her charges, including Hank and James, were looking at the roses and the five-foot-by-five-foot concrete covering over the spiral staircase entrance to the Jesus Family Tomb. Suddenly, she said to them, "I'm going to knock on the door of that apartment and explain to the occupants what we're doing so they won't be alarmed and call the police."

She walked over and saw a door bell and pushed it. Inside she could hear the tiny voice of Dinah saying to her mother, "Someone's at the door, mommy."

The older Arab said to Adina, "Answer the door, but don't say anything funny. I'll be right behind you with my finger on the button."

It was his plan to go outside after Betty and her friends were in the rose garden next to the entrance to the tomb, to walk calmly out the front door of the apartment to the side of the concrete slab and scream, "ALLAHU AKBAR" at the top of his voice and detonate the bag he held and the suicide vest at the exact moment his disciple exploded his vest, killing everyone inside the apartment. The combined explosions would then bring down the apartment house and blow a huge crater into the rose garden and explode the tomb, which would then be filled with the rubble of the destroyed apartment house.

Adina did as she was told and opened the door and said, "What can I help you with?" as she put a wild expression on her face and rolled her eyes so that no one could see except Betty. She repeated herself and rolled her eyes again.

Betty looked at her calmly and said that she and her friends were just admiring her roses and didn't want her to worry, noting that there were two men inside who were overdressed for the weather.

Adina said calmly while making the same wild expressions and rolling her eyes toward the two men, "Okay," and then closed the door.

She walked over to Hank, James, and Christopher who were standing off to the side and said, "Something strange is going on in that apartment. I think there's a guy in there with a suicide vest and he's holding a mother with her two children hostage."

As soon as she said that she noticed two Mossad agents alongside the apartment next to the stairs motioning Betty to come talk with them.

Betty and Christopher walked over to them and introduced themselves.

David, the one who motioned to her, said, "There are two guys in there ready to blow the apartment building and we just found out you are MI5." Pointing to Christopher, he continued, "Is he MI5 too?"

She replied, "No, but he'll do!"

"Do you have a gun?" he said.

"No."

"Here take mine," David said as he handed her his Walther .380 PPK with a grip laser sight. He pulled out an IWI Jericho 941 9mm pistol with a grip laser sight, handed it to Christopher, turned to his fellow Mossad agent and said, "Give me your backup. These two and I are going in with Betty and Christopher."

His buddy whispered back, "Mazel tov!"

The Mossad agents had gotten notification from a next door neighbor that she thought something strange had been going on in the apartment next to hers and she had heard strange voices of men speaking in Arabic.

Everyone was in fear over the recent terror attacks by jihadists and she was no exception. She thought it strange that her friend had not come over for lunch with her children as they usually did so she called the police who contacted the Mossad because of the possibility of terrorists.

Betty and her friends had come down the stairway before the police had cordoned off the neighborhood and just before the Mossad agents were about to enter the apartment from a service entrance they had found in the back of the apartment.

Now David and his fellow Mossad agent, Chaika, with Betty and Christopher, silently entered the apartment through the service entrance and made their way forward to the living room.

David peeked inside, came back and said, "There are two of them, one on the couch next to the mother and her two children, and the other next to the door.

"Betty, you and Chaika take the guy on the couch. Christopher, you and I are going to take out the guy at the door. He's holding a bag of explosives in one hand and the other hand on the doorknob. I'll hit his shoulder holding the bag and you and Betty go for head shots. Okay?

"When I count three—we go. Mazel tov!"

The four of them held the muzzles of their guns down as they clicked on the laser sights. A thin red beam streamed out, just like in Star Wars.

"Okay, one…two…three!"

The three of them moved swiftly through the door before anyone knew what was happening, locked their laser sights onto their targets, and pulled the triggers simultaneously. The two men dropped like bags of concrete, not knowing what had hit them.

The children and their mother screamed and then David, Betty, and Christopher went over to hug them and console with soft words Adina, Ariel, and Dinah. Everyone was sobbing with tears rolling down their cheeks when Chaika, David's Mossad buddy came through the front door as Natalie,

Dietrich, Hank, James, Allen, and Randall gathered outside to see what had happened. Hank and James saw the suicide vests and the sack of C-4 and moved in quickly to help Chaika disarm and neutralize the explosives.

"Whew! That was close," Hank proffered and James said, "Amen to that, brother!"

Chaika turned to his fellow officers, Hank, James, David, and Betty and they all hugged each other and their recruited agent, Christopher.

The operation had gone off like clockwork and the captives, neighbors, and the Tomb of the Jesus Family was saved!

27 EPILOGUE:
WHAT NEXT?

Everyone was back at MacIntosh Manor and Allen had joined them. He was amazed at the manor house even though he lived in a Frank Lloyd house and was neighbors and friends with the Roods at Point Venture on Lake Travis outside Austin, Texas.

He told them that he was absolutely in love with their new house in Scotland, but quipped, "It's not quite Saint Sophia…but close." Then he hugged Carolyn and asked her where the chocolate chip cookies were.

Kira had observed all of this and ran over to Allen and said, "Me too! Me too!"

He laughed, leaned over and said, "Me too," and kissed her on the forehead.

She was delighted.

Rania and Anton were standing off to the side listening to Dietrich, Randall, and Christopher exaggerating on their adventures.

Steve and Katie were standing next to Rania and Anton when Katie blurted out, "There has been some adventure here as well." She then looked at Rania and said, "Well, tell everyone."

Anton blushed as Rania held his hand and announced, "I'm going to have a baby...maybe two!"

Everyone grew silent to let it sink in and then in unison yelled, "Congratulations!"

After the excitement, hugging and handshaking, and asking for cigars from Anton who didn't smoke and didn't quite understand the suggestion, Carolyn calmly said, "You know, I've noticed that after these adventures, someone is always getting pregnant. I don't think I would recommend these dangerous adventures as a means of inducing pregnancy."

Christopher grinned, looked at Carolyn and then Steve and Katie and said, "You know, there's still the treasure on those other ships that went to New Jerusalem, and to quote our good friend, Dietrich here...."

He paused, and as he said the words, he looked Katie and Steve squarely in the eyes, and said, "I think the games afoot again, my dear Watson!"

28 ABOUT THE AUTHORS

FRANK R. FAUNCE

 Frank R. Faunce, DDS, is a retired colonel in the United States Army. He was an associate professor and department chair at Emory University School of Dentistry in Atlanta, Georgia. He was the command dental surgeon of the Third United States Army and served overseas in that capacity in most of the Middle Eastern countries and in East Africa. He was commissioned as a captain during the Vietnam War and was activated for duty during Operation Desert Storm. His last assignment overseas was in Mogadishu, Somalia.

Dr. Faunce completed his residency in pediatric dentistry at the University of Texas Dental Branch in Houston. He served as deputy director of the Dental Division of the Academy of Health Care Sciences at Fort Sam Houston in San Antonio, Texas, and on special assignment to the United States Army Institute for Dental Research at Walter Reed Army Hospital in Washington, DC. He also has been a consultant to Congress for Technology Assessment. He commanded the 333rd Medical Detachment in Savannah, Georgia, and has been awarded the Meritorious Service Medal with 3 Oak Leaf Clusters and the Presidential Order of Military Medical Merit.

He has written many scientific papers and articles and a textbook on aesthetic dentistry, and was a consultant to the American Dental Association on aesthetic dentistry. He was president of the Academy of Dentistry International and is a Fellow of the International College of Dentists, the American

College of Dentists, the European Academy of Prosthetics, and American Academy of Pediatric Dentistry. He has several patents and has lectured extensively at universities in the United States, Canada, Mexico, Europe and Asia. He is a Distinguished Alumnus of Indiana University School of Dentistry and Marion High School in Marion, Indiana, and Honorary Citizen of New Orleans.

Dr. Faunce's military experience and travels throughout Europe and North America provided the background for this timely novel that is replete with vivid imagery that gives the reader a sense of being there. He is now working on the sequels to *The Seton Secret*.

JOE C. RUDÉ III

Joe C. Rudé III, MD, grew up in Austin, Texas, and attended the University of Texas. While there, he won the Texas State Judo Championship and became a second-degree black belt. After medical school and internship, he joined the United States Air Force and served in Vietnam as a flight surgeon, flying 48 combat missions as the weapons systems officer in the back seat of F-4 Phantoms. For this he was awarded the Air Medal with two Oak Leaf Clusters.

After a radiology residency and fellowship at Emory University, Dr. Rudé practiced diagnostic and interventional radiology for 37 years in Atlanta, Georgia. During that time, he was elected chief-of-staff and was appointed to the Board of Trustees of one of his hospitals and served as a clinical associate professor at both the Emory University School of Medicine and the School of Dentistry. Dr. Rudé has been a member of many medical societies including being a Fellow of the Royal Society of Medicine and an Honorary Fellow of the Academy of Dentistry International.

Always an inveterate traveler with experience in scuba diving and mountaineering, Dr. Rudé was accepted as a Fellow of the Explorer's Club in New York and has participated in ten Flag Expeditions from the Andes Mountains in Peru to the highlands and coral reefs of New Guinea. He is also a Fellow of the Royal Geographical Society in London. Dr. Rudé has held multiple offices in many genealogical and heraldic organizations, and was awarded several knighthoods. Since retiring he has devoted much time to writing, publishing a fine art photography book, and producing art center exhibitions.

Made in the USA
Columbia, SC
06 February 2023

11149015R00112